THE NEAR FUTURE

JOE ASHBY PORTER

The Near Future

TURTLE POINT PRESS

New York

Copyright © 2006 by Joe Ashby Porter

ISBN 1-885586-41-8 LCCN 2005926845

Design and composition by Jeff Clark
at Wilsted & Taylor Publishing Services

CONTENTS

ONE

Manatee

The story opens in late January before dawn, in Manatee, Florida, a Gulf Coast retirement village. Fog has drifted through grass and across pavement and spilled onto the pool. Most of the mobile homes rest dark and quiet on ornamental cinderblocks. At the blue trailer on Dockside Lane, however, Vincent Margiotta, seventy-nine, six two, one forty, with a lighted flashlight prods lawnmower parts behind his shed. Should the noise wake the Runkles next door, no skin off Vince. He and Lillian had lived here five years already, together then, before the Runkles moved into their white doublewide.

Like a heron Vince reads the jumble and fishes out a lawnmower blade that might do for Lillian's mower. The doors of his pickup read "Odd Jobs," with his name and phone, and he had the legend printed on business cards last month. Tinkering and repairs mostly, and he'll gladly lend this sort of hand today to Lillian, who has moved out and left him in the lurch. Never mind if she won't have any of the other assistance Vince provides for Manatee widows and wives and spinsters. Never mind, he thinks, old Lil may yet come to her senses. Vince lodges the flashlight between his thighs, points a finger into the beam, and balances the blade across it.

Sightlines cross the dark from Vince to a window in the whitish hump starting to loom above its picket fence. The lines run through screen wire and glass and past a perfumed finger that has lifted a cream vinyl slat.

"Tsk." Gwendolyn Runkle lets the slat snap shut and interlaces her fingers under her chin. "Mr. Margiotta, of course." Gwen rotates and glides across plush in the thinning dark toward the queen-size bed where Brent Runkle sits. Silent fragrance lubricates Gwen's hems and her scuffs, both of a heavy ivory satin. "You may need to speak to him, or we might bring the matter before the village council. He's more thoughtless than ever since Lillian left him."

As Gwen passes the cherry grandmother clock she and Brent have reconditioned, it begins pealing six with a triple-chime Whittington melody, and other soft chimes and cuckoos sound through the doublewide. "Suppose we had taken him for a prowler. Yesterday at Hair Now I heard about two break-ins in December, in deluxes. No hope of recovery.

The officers said the virtuals and games were probably already plugged in in Micronesia. Oh dear heaven, I don't like to complain, but . . ." Gwen pauses at her vanity for a squirt of lotion.

Brent can almost see his wife slide toward the bed. "I understand, dear. I have a good fix on what you mean, in many ways. But all the same, you know?" Brent's forearms in striped pajama sleeves rest on the sheet.

Creaming her elbows, Gwen continues, "Sometimes I still wonder whether we shouldn't have stayed on in Memphis. Even after . . ." Gwen's eyes and Brent's wheel toward the far wall, where in a cypress frame hangs a veiled photograph of their estranged daughter at her Austin Peay graduation.

Brent shrugs. "We'll never have that one scoped."

"It's only that . . ."

Brent nods. "We've always dreamed of twilight years as a reward for our service, mine to retail shoes, yours to Drug War Mothers, all your tireless devotion and hindsight." Four eyes again wheel toward the far wall. Brent ahems. "What's done is done, though, and we mustn't let nostalgia overtake us. Might just as well mourn the Internet meltdown. I'll put a bug in Margiotta's ear. So be a good girl and tell me what today is."

Gwen slips in beside Brent. "This," she whispers, "is the first day of the rest of our lives." From the powder room trills a last Tyrolean woodnote. Silent in their wide bed, hands clasped under the sheet, the Runkles take heart. Across the wheat shag carpet, the blond and pastel settee in its polyethylene slipcover, the quilted control panels, the vintage cell phone on its tasseled cushion, and across the Runkles, light increases by insensible degrees, relentlessly.

While Lillian Margiotta's ex whets a blade, swaddles it in the army blanket in the bed of his pickup, climbs in and backs across rosy puddles, two miles away Lillian wakes. After a pit stop during which she winds her silver and black pigtail into a bun and blackens her eyelids, she shuffles to her tiny kitchen, her smallest since her and Vince's first Lower East Side one in fifty-two, smaller even than the one she left Vince with three months ago.

Lillian's new trailer is in fact a miniature version of Vince's, and Lillian likes that fine. Less to sweep and dust. Furthermore, at seventy-two it seems right for each new home to be smaller than the one before, in an orderly progress to the smallest. Elbows on skank Formica, Lillian sips Medaglia d'Oro like absinthe and hears Vince's pickup grind around the corner to a stop.

Lillian likes Manatee, no reason leaving Vince should make her leave the village. She had her eye on this trailer from the first, and when its owner left to meet his maker, Lillian pounced. Back from the realtor with the contract in her ostrich clutch, amethysts on to celebrate, Lillian called it quits with Vince and hasn't lost a wink of sleep over it since.

Rattle rattle at the door. I mean, this isn't some Brooklyn tenement like the one Vince grew up in before doorbells were invented, garbage in the street and laundry out back, wop undershirts. Cool his heels if he can't act civilized. Lillian opens the cub refrigerator. The doorbell's a small thing, you might say, except you spend decades trying with zero success to teach a man to use one—and a cabby if anybody should know how to summon someone correctly, and he can push elevator buttons, can't he?

Or these bread-and-butter pickles. Lillian lifts out the

squat Vlasic jar and nudges the fridge door shut. She sets the jar on the table in front of her and tries the top. No dice, but Vince is not what's needed. He's no Joe Palooka anymore.

Lillian opens the table drawer and takes out an instrument designed for these eventualities. She grips the jar between her knees, attaches the Jar Jif, and breaks the seal with no sweat. Her mouth starts to water. She extends her tongue and lays one tart sweet wafer on it. Vince wants sours and so for fifty years Lillian has eaten bread-and-butters only at weddings and wakes. Now she can buy them for herself. Another small thing, but at seventy-two you don't hold your breath for biggies.

Rattle rattle. "It's me, Lil, open up in there. You still with us?"

"Hold your horses," shouts Lillian. Pickles capped and back in the fridge, she strolls to the front door.

After a moment Vince says, "I found your mower a blade." He bounces it on his palm.

"Okay." The sky seems huge, with the fresh Gulf breeze and the neighboring trailers set back from Lillian's. No planes, no boats, freeway barely audible. "Okay, thanks,

Vince. I'd forgotten." Grass bends in waves from the lilac bougainvillea to the street. "You want a coffee?"

"Sure. Then I'll put the blade on, and the lawn should be dry enough for me to mow."

"So come in then. Don't bump your head. I'll make another pot."

"You don't have any more of those anise biscotti?" says Vince in the kitchen, legs stretched into the dining-living area. "You know, Lil, I was thinking. How about if you came back on a trial basis. One day at a time, no big commitment. Know what?"

"What's that?"

"How's about you pack an overnight bag while I cut your grass. You won't regret it. I've even arranged a nice surprise for you today. Have a heart, Lil." Somewhere outside a dog arfs. The Margiottas sip from the everyday demitasses and regard each other. Vince clears his throat. "In all the years, Lil, I don't think I ever told you about the first picture I fell in love with. Who knows why she was on Aunt Cecilia's wall, but there she was, black eyes and eyebrows, in a white peignoir, wringing her hands, hair loose."

"Why'd you flip?"

"Search me. Aunt Cecilia's eyebrows were darker, thicker anyway, and her bosoms had more character whenever I got a glimpse."

"Maybe the hands?"

"Nahh. But did I ever tell you, Lil, when I first saw you at that dance I says, 'A tragedienne'? Because you had the same Duse eyes as that photo. Still have."

"Okay, Vinnie. You were the cat's meow too, but give us a break."

"Steady there. A girl of a certain age shouldn't turn up her nose at compliments." Vince tosses back the last of his coffee.

Lillian drains hers. "Burn in hell. Did you go for your dental check-up?"

"You yours?"

Lillian nods: run of the mill, no particular horrors this time.

"Same here," says Vince. "He hadn't heard we'd split. So is it a deal? I'll give you the keys to the pickup in case you change your mind. One day at a time. Say," he says, swinging open the little refrigerator door, "what kind of pickles are you stocking now?"

Lillian shakes her head. "I always coveted those in the supermarkets. I put up with what I thought were the facts of life, all those years."

"They're embalmed in sugar. You might as well eat candy."

"See? That's the point. If I preferred candy that's what I'd damn well be buying. These are our waning years. I've thought about it and I plan to enjoy some things. I hadn't realized how expensive they are though, pickles, for what they are."

"So pamper yourself, but there are bigger questions. Also, you pamper yourself too long you'll be dead."

Lillian shakes her head again. "So what if I'm dead. I will be, whatever."

Vince sighs. "Lil, the unexamined life is not worth living."

She snorts. "You're quoting again. Holy mother of god, it sounds stupid too. Manzoni, Shakespeare, I don't care who it was. Not worth living? Get outta here."

Vince changes tack. "Heard from either of our girls lately? Listen, scoot your tail back where it belongs, and neither of them will learn how their mother misplaced the meaning of the word 'helpmeet.'" He rises. "I'm taking care of the lawn now. But do yourself a favor, Lil. Today's auspicious. Come on back, you'll be sorry if you don't."

Lillian looks down at her naked hands on the Formica. "Sorry is my middle name."

In a journey that began the day before, Denise Passaro and Tink Quinn plunge through Carolina, Georgia, and northwest Florida, alternating at the wheel. For both young Baltimoreans this is easily the longest journey yet taken. They pass roadblocks and prowling marauders, untouched by peril and not even altogether aware of it, they have so much to thrash out themselves. After ten months in an east Baltimore walkup neither is at all sure whether the cohabitation will continue, or should, or what the other might think about the matter.

Denise's low brow and thick dark eyebrows come from her mother, who still scrapes by in a Baltimore confectionery selling junk text and tobacco to children. Denise's freckles and slight frame come from a father who surfaced to engender her before disappearing back into the underclass. Burly Tink's freckles come from his mother, and both his parents have long since vanished.

Tink is driving the last stint of today's leg, elbow out the open window. The orange coupe weaves through moderate traffic like a princess, wiggling her tailpipes at larger, darker sedans with smoked glass and satellite links, wolves cruising three miles under the limit except when they're in a hurry. Denise navigates, a map open on her lap. Humming along with the radio's drifting salsa, she waves to road gangs and the occasional hitchhiker. Denise is pleased with the Hawaiian Bermudas and shirts and the flip-flops she has bought Tink and herself for their midwinter whee in the Sunshine State. She found them and the sunscreen and the colored mirror shades, hers peacock, his bronze, in a Baltimore thrift store.

"Look there." Tink points with a pinky. The bridge seems to be crossing a salt marsh, with remains of an earlier parallel bridge visible above the water. On pilings perch dark fowl with hanging wings.

"Anhingas," says Denise. "What did we read, prehistoric, or they don't exactly fly?"

"Something like that, babe."

Bumpety bump bumpety bump over expansion joints and now a shush and splat between palms and motels. "Tink?" says Denise. "Are you glad Christmas is over? I am." She rubs a fingertip forward on the map. "I'm primed to get down to business. Even if some fun's in the cards too. I'm ready to rock and roll, and I don't see how this angle can lose. Dudes down here must like a fast buck, and we're talking serious venture capital."

"Serious as it gets."

"Right. I mean, venture capital's what keeps the whole enchilada afloat from here on."

"And above ground."

"Check. So, Tink, it looks to me like we've got it made in the shade. We have a package that what's-his-name looking for the fountain . . ."

"Corleone."

Denise nods. "He would have said forget the fountain. Who needs it if you can have untold wealth? If you've struck a gusher."

Tink steers thoughtfully. "But why give up youth if we're

talking druthers? And let's don't forget love." Tink wiggles eyebrows.

"Okay," says Denise. "Well, is there a love fountain down here too, I hope?"

Tink grins. "Gusher."

Denise's eyes mist. "Maybe they're sentries, those anhingas, that let pass only the pure in heart." She peruses the map. "This exit."

Tink peels off onto the ramp. "Wait, is this what we've come to Florida's backside for? What's the place called again?"

"Manatee. Population thirty thousand. Trust me, Tink."

Brent and Gwen Runkle have converted their mudroom into a hobby center. Noon finds Brent at the workbench equipped with outlets for wood-burning styli, buffers and grinders, and other tools used mainly by Gwen when she devises clock bodies, and equipped with the powerful light necessary for the work Brent is now engaged in, whistling with a merengue he hears over headphones, in one eye a watchmaker's loupe through which he can almost see the lubricant grains that coat gears and hands, wafer batteries and solar cells, tweezers and velvet.

Clock-making has edged out Brent's and Gwen's other hobbies through the years since the rupture with their daughter and her departure for parts unknown like a thief in the night from their Memphis hideaway, her camper stuffed not only with her own belongings but also with such treasures from the Memphis family hobby center as Gwen's semiprecious stones and smithy and Brent's chemistry set. Clock-making fills the gap left by hobbies it would be heart-breaking to resume.

Today Brent devotes himself to a genuine conversation piece, a clock that runs backward. It will hang in the dou-blewide's entryway where it will be legible in the ormolu mirror opposite. Hanging the new clock will necessitate moving photographs of pets from happier times, probably to the powder room where Miau-miau and Cuddles can somersault over the porthole.

Brent is almost as short as his wife, and he can't help oc-casionally supposing that his name inhibited growth in the years when buddies with other names shot past him. As a teenager he took his share of ribbing about size, but that didn't stop him from lettering in diving. Nor was Brent's size any problem with Gwen Ferby, far from the least popular girl in their class. At the prom, as they foxtrotted with a verve denied even the most adept of larger classmates, Brent proposed and Gwen accepted. She wrote him every day of the eighteen months he spent in Korea, letters that now nestle in camphor-soaked silk. They married the week of his return and the next week he embarked on a successful career as a retail shoe salesman.

Brent's part of the clock-making enterprise is the most essential and also the simplest. He positions the bushing in the face, mounts hands on the shaft, and inserts a battery in the quartz movement, whereupon the clock begins telling time. Brent then sets it to the U.S. atomic clock via satellite. Gwen in her turn will install the clock and bezel.

Brent sets in the concave glass, and almost immediately feels a caress on his dry neck. He pops out the loupe and turns to see Gwen with a tray of gleaming canapés. "I thought we might lunch on the veranda. The weather is adorable." At the back of Gwen's head in a net snood swings a dollop of hair colored like jar mayonnaise and as lustrous. This afternoon in a simulcast she will represent

Manatee in a teleconference of Tampa Bay concerned citizens, and she has donned a taupe jumpsuit with a flattering peplum for the occasion. Brent will swim laps, as he does three afternoons a week.

Now through the trailer a musical clamor tolls noon.

"Strangers," says Gwen, glancing under a frilly valence. "Young ones. Apparently visiting Mr. Margiotta. Which reminds me, precious, dinner at the cafeteria might be a good time to speak to him about his disruptiveness. Although it might not take if he brings that tramp with him again, that horse."

Vince Margiotta flings open the chalky aluminum door of his trailer and waves like a scarecrow. Even before the orange coupe toodles to a halt, the passenger door is opening. Out piles Denise in her island togs. "Gramps!"

"Neesy, my favorite grandchild. How long's it been?"

"Christ, Gramps, eight years, ten? My best maternal grandpa looks great too, looks just the same. How's about a hug? Over my shoulder you should be catching sight of my current better half, Tink Quinn, also of Baltimore. I didn't tell you he was coming because I wanted to surprise you. Lillian asleep? Gramps, Tink. Tink, Gramps."

"What's happening, Pops? Are those baby palms?"

"Call me Vince, son. Palmettos, some are older than you. Welcome. No trouble on the road? So, Neesy, a little surprise for you too. Lil and I are separated, three months now. We didn't want your mother to worry so we've kept quiet. Also it may not be permanent—not much down here is. You're looking swell. Not the flat-chested little Neesy I used to bounce on my knee. You kids hungry? Want a beer? Ever drink Corona up in Baltimore? There's some cheese and crackers in the kitchen, or I can microwave a pizza."

Denise shakes her head. "We pigged out up the road. But you didn't say where Lillian is. You kick her out, or she split?"

"Son—Tink, is it?—if you two are bunkmates you can take the gear all the way through, past the head. Lillian's right here in Manatee, Neesy, living by herself in a dollhouse trailer on the other side of the golf course. Her decision, and she didn't give any warning. Didn't lay down terms either. If she'd asked me to call a halt to helping Manatee widows through bereavement, I'd have taken it under advisement. But no, no conditions."

Denise raises a finger to interrupt, but Vince continues. "I don't think my charity work drove her to it, incidentally. I've been consoling the random widow since before you were born, and Lillian has certainly known some of it, even if it wasn't our breakfast table conversation."

Tink chuckles but Vince's eye is on his granddaughter. "Why is little you looking crestfallen," he wants to know, "in those sporty duds. Lillian doesn't know you're here. I hoped to have her back by now, and you'd be a surprise, but that's neither here nor there. We'll drop in this afternoon after I've given you and your boyfriend a tour of our retirement paradise. What is it, Neesy girl? I thought I had only one foot in the grave."

"Aw, you're the picture of health, Gramps. I guess I just always romanticized the two of you. I thought of you two in a golden mist down here and I wanted to impress Tink. But listen."

"Yes?"

"I was looking forward to seeing Lillian again too—wait, she is my real gram, right?"

"Realer than real."

"Then why do I call her Lillian?"

"Her doing, Neesy. Something about names. She'll let me address her as Lil but not call her that to any third party unless it's a member of the family."

"So who am I?"

"I should have said, to a member of her generation. Family you certainly are. Lillian loves you too."

"Sure," says Denise. She stands in hot windless sun like a luauer who's bitten off more than she can chew, sweat starting to glint on her white brow and on her whisper of a moustache. Denise says "Sure" as if love were a kind of joke.

Vince saws the air. "But what's the story with you and this potato head, I mean potato eater? Doesn't Baltimore have even one single Italian good enough to be my grandson-in-law? Did I raise a daughter—how is your mother, anyhow? Yes, I want to hear all about her, and don't spare me any gory detail, I'm past taking it personally—but I can't help asking myself, did I raise a daughter who'd raise a daughter to be a traitor to her own kind? Listen." Vince leans back and lays his hands over his kidneys, flapping his elbows. "There's probably nothing wrong with your Tink, but if things don't work out I know two Italian widows here in Manatee. At least one must have an unattached grandson somewhere."

Denise has been thinking. "You want Lillian back, do you?"

"Absolutely. For one thing . . ."

After a moment Denise says, "Uh, yeah, Gramps?"

Vince twists his neck to stare out over the treetops and mobile-home tops, the lower rims of his eyelids starting to droop away. He kicks a conch shell blistering at the edge of his driveway. "Well, for one thing, I'd like us to be together in our final resting places, if you get my drift. She and I've had this nice little plot waiting for us up in Jersey for thirty years and more. But don't mention it when we visit."

"About that visit, Gramps, I, uh . . ." Denise holds pink plastic in her teeth long enough to corral a barretteful of ringlets at her crown. Attached, they cascade like a mantilla. "After all, I'm not sure I want to see Lillian. I can barely remember her, skittish, opening and closing a big purse, long in the tooth. If she's treating you like dirt, Gramps, I wouldn't know how to comport myself. You needn't tell her I'm here. Tink, find the bedroom?"

Tink steps down, bow-legged and expansive. "Nice little cubbyhole you got here, Vince, real homey. Denise'll feel right at home. Toilet's nice and clean too. Looks to me like he don't need any old lady." Tink smooths back his crew cut and spreads his arms like a singer. "Vince, this is the kind of setup I've dreamed of. The village seems safe enough too. Coming in, we had to tell the monitor our destination. Me, though, I'd consider clearing out some of that tall stuff in back."

"Okay," says Vince. "Maybe I'll let you bush-hog it, Tink. So, who's up for a tour of the compound? More oldsters than you ever saw in one place together, and up to our natural tricks in a scenic habitat. Let's take your car, it'll have the airwaves humming."

Tink rubs his palms. "Sounds good. Why don't you hop in the back, Vince, and direct us. I still drive, babe?"

"Let me. Here, Gramps. Is there room for those legs of yours? I don't remember you this thin."

Tink holds the passenger door open. "How much you

weigh there, Vince? You're welcome to twenty of my pounds if we can swing a transfer."

"Make that thirty," says Denise. "And let me choose the thirty. Let's put our top down, Tinker."

"All set?" says Tink. "Okay, Neese, let her rip. Guess we can back straight onto the street—not much fast traffic around here, is there, Pops, I mean Vince. Which way did you say we should head?"

"Back past where you came in," says Vince, his long fingers over the seat backs in front of him. "That a fuzz-buster on the dash? This is a sweet little jalopy, Tink, but I don't see how you can have much security with a ragtop. Maybe you don't need it up in Baltimore."

Tink swivels to talk easier with Vince and watch Denise drive. "Don't kid yourself. It'd take an Uzi to make a dent in that fabric. Space grade windows too, and the body's a new industrial composite. Plus there's motion sensors and sirens. Baltimore's not Florida but you gotta take precautions up there too. Right, Neesy?"

Vince points. "What's that beneath the tachometer?"

"Raises and lowers a persuader under the hood. I don't believe in arming civilian vehicles but, hey, the best offense is a good defense. You book around Manatee in that pickup?"

"Little as possible. When I turned in my hack permit in seventy-three I told Lillian she could do our driving from then on—I'd spent enough of my life behind the wheel. Hang a left." Vince pats Denise's left shoulder.

"So where'd you drive a cab, and for how long?" asks Tink as Denise hangs a smooth left onto an avenue leading to water.

"Manhattan Island," says Vince. "Center of the universe, or so it seemed then. For more years than you are old, maybe twice as many."

"Like it?"

Denise chimes in, "Yeah, you recommend it, Gramps?"

Vince says, "Stop here and idle a minute, Neesy. Those are the town docks, and over there are berths and moorings. Through there to the main canal, which gives onto Tampa Bay."

"Got a boat yourself?" asks Tink.

"Couldn't pay me," says Vince. Herons, anhingas, pelicans, gulls, and terns, perched on posts and rails of the docks and on masts and lines of boats riding at anchor, eye the coupe. Near the water's edge two small alligators sun themselves on the boat ramp.

"Cripes," says Denise. "Would you look at that!"

Vince nods. "They're not real. We just keep them there to scare the gulls off, so the ramp doesn't get too slimy."

Tink says, "But there must be some real ones around if shills scare the birds." A breeze wrinkles the surface of the water. "Are there?"

"Yes indeedy," says Vince.

"Ever see one?"

"I think I did once. In a canebrake back of a widow's yard I was mowing, but it might have been a log. You're never sure until it's too late."

"Gramps!" says Denise in a mock reprimand. "How many widows' yards do you mow down here?"

"Twelve or fifteen," says Vince. "They're not all widows either. Anyhow, cabbying wasn't bad, for an Italian that didn't make it past tenth grade."

"How'd you manage that?" says Tink. "Truant officer on the take?"

"I just didn't go back. Lit out one August on a Greyhound headed west. My plan was to work my way around the world to Bermuda and then settle down in a thatched hut long enough to get to know some of those hibiscus girls I thought the island must be crawling with, and to write a newspaper story about my travels. I stepped off the bus in Sauk Center, Minnesota, and found a job sweeping in a hotel barbershop and running errands for the barbers and customers.

"I lived in the attic of a men's boardinghouse. A Norwegian widow ran it and did the cooking, served pudding every meal, especially bread pudding. There was me, a bank teller, a schoolteacher, a mailman, and a shoe drummer when he was in town, none over thirty. We had good times shooting the bull at the table about politics or whatever, religion, in those days some young people took those things for real. Not me, but lots."

Tink shrugs and turns down the corners of his mouth. Denise sits with thumbs hooked over the bottom of the steering wheel. The engine coughs and she gives it a gentle gun.

Vince continues, "After four or five months I'd saved enough and was pulling up stakes to head on to Frisco. It was my last day at the barbershop and a telegram comes for me. My sainted mother had finally kicked the bucket—Papa had shown her how a year before—and the older brothers and sisters wanted me to come back to watch over the two youngest boys until they could take care of themselves. So." Vince's hands wave out over the orange fenders. "So goodbye Tahiti and the Taj Mahal, goodbye Sphinx, goodbye Paree and those Bermuda wahines. So long, journalistic fame. See you later, I thought I was saying, but it turned out to be addio. Three years later an uncle bonded me for the hack license and another uncle lent me enough for Lillian's diamond.

"Okay, Neesy, right at the bus shelter, hug the shore long as you can and then hang another right just past the wall. People will stare but the sight of me will save you from lynching."

The three pile out and cross the blacktop past salmon bougainvillea and openly skeptical grannies and grampses to the low-slung social hall. Inside in an echoing half-light Vince shows the sign-up sheets. "Anything you want, just give her your John Hancock. You bowl? There's the dance floor." Dimpled black-and-white linoleum on concrete, bleachers under high windows. At the far end rises a modest stage where, Vince explains, Tuesdays at the mike that resembles him he calls square dance. "Ahh-lemand left and a doe-see-doe and a hippy-hop high and a wiggly-worm low. Fuhh-ling-a you partner, don't be shy, when the cows a-come a-home a-then so shall I."

"Gramps?" asks Denise. "That Norwegian pudding widow, was she a corrupter of youth, if you follow?"

Vince shakes his head. "Mrs.—what was her name?—was the one got corrupted. She said I was her only man besides her dead husband, and I believe it was the truth. She never smiled. I remember looking down between her plump knees at that dour face. She had earmuff braids and a lantern jaw, and she always frowned like she disapproved of what we were doing. One time I saw tears running down under the braids, and so I stopped, er, moving, and I says, 'Beg pardon, Mrs. Rasmussen, we must be hurting you.' I was still a little wet behind the ears where all that's concerned, so I just braked and asked her flat out like that. Rasmussen she was, I never knew her given name. Maybe Gretl.

"Well, so here's where I call square dances. Lillian deejays and most of the first Tuesday after she walked out on me I spent here learning to operate the CD player and coordinate calls and patter. Come seven, after I'd gone home for a can of beans and duded up, I walks in and there cool as a cucumber at her regular place sits Lillian. Barely notices me. The civic association bought the CD player used from a grandkid, and we get a senior discount for the disks. We have ballroom dancing Saturday nights, aerobics every morning, bridge some afternoons, bingo some, monthly town meetings, memorial services for residents that croak. Dartboard, checkers and chess.

"Okay, that's it for the social hall. We can walk across and see the game room, and on the way look in at the 'Library.' Oh, and could you sign the guest register?"

As Tink writes in trim block capitals, Denise asks, "Grampsy, though, about Ms. Rasmussen. It was thoughtful of you to ask if the balling was causing her discomfort, but you forgot to say what she said. Or maybe you didn't forget exactly."

"I'd tell you if I could," says Vince. "When I said, 'We seem to be hurting you,' Mrs. Rasmussen shook her head from side to side, eyes still closed, and then she said something Norwegian in a real low voice. Then she, ah, gave me to understand that she wanted me to get back down to business. It would be worth learning Norwegian to find out what she said, if only I could remember it. She must be pushing up daisies now."

Halfway to the game room squats the "Library." Vince guides his young charges through a bunkerlike door into a cocoon of hologram screens and weak light where they may finger "books" and sit on an extruded sofa under a hanging shaded lamp to address a reference console. Then the trio proceeds toward the game room, past the Olympic pool where a lone brown swimmer upends in mid-lap to wave.

Vince clasps hands over his head like a champion. "How many so far?"

"You said it," calls Brent. He waves again and resumes the horizontal, to continue his crawl through the bright water.

"Brent's hearing's not what it once was," says Vince, striding away from the pool toward an adobe and pink stucco building. "He and his missus live next door—you'll meet them at dinner. Okay, here we are." Discreet blue neon announces "GAMES" under a brooding lintel. Vince pauses with a foot on the first step. "Retirement village game rooms can be tamer than outside. Still, till somebody locates an

OIDS cure, we oldsters need our own amenities. We got booths, video hookups, diddlers, and of course we got the regular public games too, that I can show you."

"Speaking of OIDS there Vince," says Tink, massaging his chin, "I'm assuming you take precautions with your lady friends."

Denise dabs her twinkling brow with a hankie. "I was thinking the same thing, Gramps."

Vince eyes the youngsters beneath him. "Could it be the cash cow up your sleeve Neesy mentioned in her last letter has something to do with such matters?" He cocks a brow and waits.

Denise and Tink search each other and shrug. Palms rattle outside.

"No? At your age I thought everything had to do with such matters. Then time passed, and I re-prioritized somewhat. Anyway don't expect to see geezers with their tooties out in the game room. The booths lock from inside."

"What if a geezer . . ." Denise wants to know.

"Croaks, or starts to? Hey, we're twenty-first-century state of the art here. A gamester can have a high old time at the screen safe in the knowledge that, except for the usual, erratic behavior, including simple stasis, gets noticed through the electric eye in the back of the booth. A bonded concierge overrides the lock and sounds alarms. Nice of you to ask, though."

Half a mile east of the activity complex behind a faded caboose thunk, thunk goes the hoe of a tall spinster in gumshoes, overalls, a sailor jersey, and a deep sunbonnet, Vola Byrd. Thunk thunk, *crang* on a rock, thunk thunk to the end of a row turned for winter parsley. "Whew!" Vola skins off her bonnet, tosses it and the hoe against a cinderblock wall, and turns back to appraise the truck garden with her famous Windex eyes.

For most of her sixty-eight years Vola Byrd has eaten a good bunch or two of parsley a week. "Heavy on the parsley, hon," she instructed waiters during her Manhattan years in the real estate fast lane. Now that reverses have landed her here in a leaky Flagler Railroad relic on an 18 × 60 lot, scraping by with a miserly pension, parsley's one thing Vola won't scrimp on, even though getting her fill under budget means hopping clods like her mother in Oklahoma the better part of a century ago. First thing tomorrow,

Vola will cast seed and turn it under. She could have bought plugs, but transplanting parsley's unlucky. Leastwise it probably would be to Vola.

Inside, horizontal Gulf light floods the caboose. Vola sits on a lower bunk to slide long white feet out of her boots. Clum, sounds an empty boot on gray pine almost petrified with age, clum the other, flackle flackle the pair as Vola's naked heels hustle them under. She steps across to a wicker hamper beside a wicker telephone table under a gaggle of clothes hangers on a pipe. Humming a snatch of national anthem like an electric oboe, Vola sheds her remaining clothing and lets it slide or billow into the hamper. Oodle oodle oodle sounds the phone. Vola barely glances at the caller's number before she brushes past into the bathroom and activates the shower.

Bending to position her head lower than the showerhead to wet her silver bob with soft Manatee water, Vola reflects anew on the cruelty of her present pickle. If only Silicon Valley hadn't popped, if only bin Laden had had second thoughts. Vola turns, fills a palm with golden shampoo, and suds it. Vola M. Byrd, having clambered up from the Okie dustbowl to the highest reaches of Trump Tower, now bends to rinse under a rusted shower head in an abandoned caboose plunked onto a postage stamp abutting the zoom zoom freeway audible even under the spray.

Vola who, without benefit of matrimony or any helpmeet for longer than a few weeks max, made herself a real estate name that was reckoned with as recently as twenty months back, a name that stood under sixteenth-page aerial views in the Sunday *Times* magazine through two decades, now rises from under the misting needles and shakes back her gray in an aqua nook the very gardener's wife on one of the estates she has marketed would turn up a nose at. Vola soaps the loofah that came with her to Manatee because no Queens passerby made an offer for it on the sidewalk outside the apartment that marked the last stage of her precipitous New York decline. She reaches over to scrub wide shoulder blades and their valley and then turns, "Whoops!," losing the soap bar but cornering it against the fiberglass before it can skitter out of reach. Spray against shoulders, she slides her left forearm under her breasts and lifts them to expose the ribcage beneath for the loofah, and somehow finds herself saying, "Easy come, easy go," even though in truth neither was easy and only the going was fast.

Toweling down on the mat, Vola says the line again. Might it give her a rakish appeal? Because now for the first time it may be necessary to consider such matters. Vola who for decades expected to retire to a Riverside Drive penthouse knows that unless something changes she'll be turned out of this very caboose before the year's end. And Vola M. Byrd has no desire to wind up selling matches to crackheads under a bridge.

Drying, Vola steps nude to her lingerie drawer, where she begins to gird herself for a social evening of the sort available to a woman of a certain age in reduced circumstances. At her makeshift vanity she lays aside her tortoiseshell bifocals and, nose nearly against the mirror, does her eyes. She replaces the bifocals with a rueful glance at the case that holds her last set of disposable contacts.

On a rack beside the hamper waits Vola's small collection of large shoes, tartan bedroom slippers, beaded moccasins, black patent flats, low yellow duck slingbacks, and white pinked kid opera heels. She sets the last onto the floor and steps into them. She slips a white rayon shift with a ruffled scalloped capelet over her head and zips it. Another run-through of the comb, behind each ear a spot of bargain simulacrum of her glory days' scent, and . . . Vola frowns. She bends to peer out the caboose's west window. Pottle pottle wheeze, around Vola's gatepost and up her driveway chugs an unfamiliar coupe the very color of the flaming sky. It stops and out piles a pair of young extras from a Hawaii rerun. Vola frowns more until out the back seat clambers her date Vince Margiotta. Nothing to write home about, but a girl has to eat.

"Neesy Passaro, Tink Quinn, Vola Byrd." Vince barely has room to open his arms beside Vola on the dust-colored plush of the back seat of the coupe, its canvas roof now in place. "Neesy's my favorite granddaughter, Tink's her prime squeeze. They've driven this buggy all the way from Baltimore. Planning on moving to Manatee, lowering our actuarials, ha ha. No, but kids this is the fine lady I told you about. New resident, hasn't really had time to learn to appreciate yours truly's finer points yet. Couple miles down the access, Neptune's, but they have meat too. Best cafeteria on the coast, some say."

"Welcome to Florida, kids," says Vola. "First time?"

Denise turns and smiles, appraising. "Hi."

"Hi there, Vola," says Tink into the rear-view mirror. "Right, first time south of Foggy Bottom."

Denise continues, "Vola, I admire you for being able to go out with a married man. Tink's not married but I've dated married guys before."

"Good for you, Neesy," says Vola. "I guess."

Denise pushes hair away from her brow. "Marriage doesn't mean what it used to. Plus I've never been particularly close to Vince's wife. Vince is my favorite grandparent. Ever visit Baltimore?"

Vola nods. "Years ago, when people traveled more. I spent my productive years in Manhattan and sometimes some of us went down to Baltimore for what we called a bad weekend. Hootchie kootchie on the Strip."

"Not that Manhattan was exactly a den of innocence," observes Vince.

"No, and in fact then—and heaven knows now—you could find anything Baltimore had to offer in Manhattan. You just would have needed passwords, maybe references. Baltimore let it all hang out, so it felt more wicked."

"A sure sign of the opposite, huh?" says Tink.

Vola nods. "Had some good times, sipping stingers and

watching Blaze Starr or Ruby Montana. Real good fun. Maybe you kids learned about those days in your history classes. That was before OIDS, before AIDS even, and back then drugs weren't, well, you understand."

Tink slows and eases onto the drive. Vola continues, "Crunch, crunch. Mmm, tires on gravel. This cafeteria must be okay with so many cars already. You don't hear this crunch in Manhattan, Baltimore either, I guess. For me, thanks, Tink, getting out's never as easy as getting in, for me that crunch always sounds like money, because I only heard it at clients' estates. You young folks go ahead, you need sustenance more. What do you recommend, Vince, the fish?"

"Everything. I've never been disappointed."

"It does all look good enough to eat, doesn't it, Tink," says Vola. "Makes you wish you had a snake's belly and could scarf down a month's worth."

Vince leans forward to speak across Vola in the line to Tink. "This is on me, dude, by the way."

Denise leans over her tray to speak back across Tink and Vola. "No indeedy, Gramps. It's on us. We're not living on fixed incomes and we insist. Chow down and bear it."

Vola touches her tray in front of the luscious entrees at

their steam table. She taps her right toe against her left heel, deciding. With a shrug of her eyebrows she glances up at Vince.

"Just this once, then," he mutters. He leans back to address Tink across Vola's ruffles. "Speaking of income, I hope your boondoggle doesn't have anything to do with," Vince glances at the dark-skinned servers, and behind him in the line at three tanned matrons, "with pharmaceuticals."

Tink leans back to say, "Ha ha, there, Vince." He turns to consult Denise about the molded salads. At the register he lingers to settle up while she follows a tuxedo to a reserved table in a raised corner alcove.

Vince introduces the remains of his party to Conchita the cashier, who manages to welcome Vola as if she were Vince's first lady guest at Neptune's while at the same time leaving Vola with an unspoken suggestion that others may have preceded her.

"Lovely to make your acquaintance, dear," Vola tells Conchita, and then slides a heaped steaming tray off the runners and proceeds like a priestess between the tables toward the dais where Denise waves and two strangers smile.

Midway in her progress Vola pauses to lay the mock golf tongue of her right shoe across the back of her left ankle as she leans back and asks Vince over her shoulder, "Who are the munchkins with your niece?"

"Brent and Gwen, neighbors. They usually join us here for Thursday dinners." Vince thinks he hears Vola murmur " 'Us'?" as she resumes her deliberate advance across the distressed carpet. He chuckles.

Introductions performed, Gwen explains to Vola that the mere two-foot elevation of the dais seems to allow dinner conversation to unfold at its own pace above the din. "Brent and I favor Neptune's because you're more apt to find retirees, but at these prices it's hard to keep out families with children. Of course some retirees at dinner resemble children."

"Grabby?"

"And loud. But up here we feel able to carry on civilized conversations. How are your salmon patties, dear? And your rib-eye, and, what's that, a veal cutlet?"

"Yum City," says Vola.

Brent nods encouragingly. "Every time we come here it

pleases us more. Pepito the chef is a personal friend—we golf, and Gwen burnt him a clock face we'll enjoy on our way out. He's in our Optimists' too. Cuban, wears Brazilian loafers even in the kitchen, that he gets for a song through some kind of connection. I used to be a shoe salesman. Ahem," says Brent when Gwen's tiny chin directs his attention to Vince. "Vince, my man. Up bright and early this morning, weren't we! Spiffing digs up for these youngsters?"

Vince flaps one hand toward the Baltimoreans and one toward Brent. "I'm okay for odd jobs but I need a live-in housekeeper. I did get the bed made, I think."

"And put out towels," Denise informs the assembly. "Plus, there's a nice big bouquet on the coffee table."

"Bougainvillea, courtesy of the Community Center."

Gwen's eyebrows rise. "Courtesy?"

Vince grins. "In a manner of speaking."

"Those teeth yours there, Vince?" asks Tink.

"Absolutely. Not store-bought, either."

"What I thought, man," Tink confides. "More than I can say for myself, by the way. These two here are on a bridge."

"Neesy do that to you?" asks Vince. "By the way, Tink, could you be any relation to Carmel Quinn? Good singer even if she wasn't Italian. I used to hear her on Arthur Godfrey when I was driving my cab. He was Irish too, wasn't he? He treated her better than our Italian singers. Oh well, that's history, and you youngsters probably never heard of Julius La Rosa."

Denise and Tink shrug at each other.

"He had a big voice," Brent offers. "Not rap or salsa, mind you. More bel canto."

"Still living?" asks Vola.

Vince shakes his head.

"OIDS?"

Vince shakes his head. "Old age neither, muggers neither. I think I read where a cardiac got him. Julius La Rosa sang good enough for opera, if you ask me. But say, kids, you got something against our seafood? Listen, red tide doesn't make it into the Gulf."

Gwen smiles modestly, her face agleam. "We don't have much trouble with medical wastes either."

"No," says Denise, "I just wanted to try something new.

I've never had chicken croquettes. I think I like them better than McNuggets. Different. Tink always eats meatloaf when we go out, if they have it."

"Besides," Tink adds, "Baltimore has a crab house on every corner."

"Vince, sugar," says Vola, "I think my eyes were bigger than my stomach. Could we ask for a doggie bag? Where'd you drive taxi, by the way?"

"Manhattan, with the occasional fare into the boroughs when I was in the mood."

"You don't mean it. I wonder if I ever rode with you. I lived on West End near Eighty-second for thirty years and did real estate all over, the island, Long Island, Short Hills, upstate. Wouldn't it be funny. I was younger, of course."

"Everybody was," says Vince. "I'd remember you though."

"Our crab houses aren't fixed up this nice," says Denise, eyeing the fishnets draped from buoy to buoy, the starfish and lanterns.

"Better class of clientele too," adds Tink. "I guess you don't have too many rumbles here."

"Not as a rule," concurs Gwen with a sniff.

"Not with this security," says Tink, canting his forehead toward a scanning camera. "I noticed them in the lot, too."

Vince stands. "Coffee?"

"Regulars for Tink and me, Gramps."

"Decaf for Gwen and me. She needs all the sleep she can get. Even with earplugs, the littlest noise wakes her."

"Better than a watchdog," observes Vince. "You can see why I sleep like a baby, with Gwen Runkle next door. Vola?"

"Decaf. And could you bring me a slice of that key lime pie? I'd love a taste. Must be a Florida specialty. I've never had a chance to sink my teeth into any."

"Yes," Gwen explains, "it originated in the Keys. Before refrigeration and irradiation inhabitants called conchs ate mainly seafood, and could have survived on it, I suppose, but they seem to have felt a need for pie. They had always sucked native limes for scurvy, and someone realized they could be used in pie. The flesh is yellower and sweeter. Flour kept and so did lard, and they had eggs, but milk was the question. Well, somebody thought of using canned sweetened condensed milk."

Brent adds, "It has its own mystique like any local dish. Green's ersatz. Ever visit the Keys?"

Vola shakes her head.

Gwen continues, "We haven't either. Some say you have to go there for the authentic version, but Neptune's's is nothing to sneeze at. I think you'll find it rich and silky. Are you enjoying the Flagler caboose, by the way? I'm told it was in its present location when the original developer acquired the land for Manatee."

"Flagler?" asks Denise.

"Henry M.," says Vince. "These are decafs and here, Vola, pie. Flagler built a railroad to Key West. Opened in the teens. The thirty-five hurricane demolished it but they say pieces still stand."

"That blow was a doozey," offers Brent.

Tink nudges Denise. "In school we had a disaster awareness day for one that hit Miami or wherever. We sent canned goods to the homeless. Milk, in fact."

Gwen rotates. "Kids, don't concern yourselves, or you either, Vola. This is the safe season, and this part of Florida is safer than some."

"Too bad about the railroad," says Denise. "How many died building it, five hundred? We did some reading before we left Baltimore."

"Seven," says Tink. "And Flagler shelled out fifty million 1906 smackers for the project. Good investment though, because he left his widow the richest woman in the country. Speaking of widows, Vola, are you one, or a divorcee? Got any children and grandchildren? You probably fessed up already, when I wasn't listening."

"Tinky," protests Denise. "Where do you get off, prying like that?"

Vola sets her empty coffee mug on St. Augustine in the turquoise Florida printed on her scalloped placemat. She cantilevers the bulk of her key lime pie into a polystyrene wedge, snaps on the cap, and slips the dish into her space-age doggie bag. "None of the above. Byrd's my maiden name and I expect to take it to the grave whether or not I marry. Vola M. Byrd, the most trusted name in fin-de-siècle Manhattan area luxe estates. Offspring never crossed my mind either." She scoots back her chair. "What, am I the last?"

"You win then," says Vince, fingers sliding through ruffles over Vola's collarbones. All others rise. "Well then Gwen, Brent, here's wishing you a fine howdy-do. Hugs and kisses all around." He leans toward his granddaughter and her beau. "At our age, you see, the weekly meeting has intrinsic value. 'Margiotta?' 'Present.' "

"I do have a matter to hash over with you, Vince," says Brent. "At your convenience."

"Whenever," says Vince, leading his party toward the crossed tridents at the exit. "We're outta here, doll," he tells Conchita the cashier. "See you next week."

"Good night, Vince," she says. "Gwen, Brent, night all. Stay outta trouble."

"Sure thing," says Brent. "Tell Pepito we voted him another star. That pirate flag clock, by the way," he explains to the youngsters and Vola, "that's one Gwen and I made."

In the parking lot the group splits with further expostulations of welcome, delight, and hope, and with mock cautions about dodging traffic on the way back to Manatee. Gwen Runkle settles into her passenger seat and Brent trots around. Beyond him the orange coupe eases over a speed bump onto the pavement under a full moon. Gwen touches open Brent's door at the security panel beside the ignition. Inside, he says, "Maybe Vince got the message, but if he makes a nuisance of himself again I'll just have to take the bull by the horns."

"Mmm."

"What is it, dear? Pensive?"

Gwen purses her lips. Brent knows to wait. At length Gwen says, "I really do wonder whether Lillian is aware how Vince is squiring strangers about in public, and the talk it's bound to cause. There hasn't been a word about divorce, has there?" Brent shrugs. "Maybe they're old-style Catholics. Or maybe they're avoiding it for the sake of . . ." He breaks off and begins whistling.

Gwen waits through a chorus of "Tannenbaum" (in mid-January, in the balmy air it takes a moment even to identify) and then says, "He doesn't seem to be sheltering his granddaughter from much. Somebody ought to inform Lillian of all this. Maybe I'll drop over tomorrow, ostensibly to see the dollhouse she's licking her wounds in."

"I'd invite you all in," says Vola as the coupe slows, "but the place looks like death warmed over. I'm in the middle of a gardening project out back. Parsley. I'll give you some, Vince, and you kids too if you're through here again. I've had to let housekeeping slide. Thanks for the hand, Neesy. No, the back seat's plenty roomy even for two giraffes like me and Vince. It's only that, am I on the porch or the running board? Here we go, oops. This evening has been a treat."

"Walk you to the door," says Vince, nosing his own knees past the tilted seat back.

"Don't bother, sugar." Vola clambers halfway back inside. "Is that my doggie bag? And thanks again for the date. Eyes forward, troops, while Vince and I do a good-night peck. Well, toodle-oo."

"Okay, Vola," says Vince. "If you insist. I was hoping to get you back to my place for a whatever while the youngsters snooze. I admit it, it's no crime. So, can I call you tomorrow?"

Vola reaches in and musses Vince's carefully distributed hair. "Not before noon, tiger—a girl needs her beauty rest. But it's been fun. I mean it."

"Night, Vola," says Denise. "Sweet dreams."

"Oh sure," breathes Vola. "Same to you, Neesy. Don't let the bedbugs bite."

"Make yourselves at home, kids. Nightcap?"

Denise walks over to slide arms around Vince's waist

from behind. "I'm bushed, Gramps. You men can chew the fat but don't push it—I want some company at breakfast. Gramps," she says as he swivels in her arms and plants kisses on both her cheeks, "why don't you come visit in Baltimore? We'd show you a good time."

"Well," says Vince.

"Seriously, think about it. Night-night."

In a moment Vince says, "Maybe you're sleepy too, Tink."

"That means you are?"

"At my age you're never sleepy. Don't even sleep much—don't seem to need it. So tell me how this cash cow of yours works. And let's raid the Margiotta cellars." Vince roots under a window seat. "Chestnuts in syrup, orange-flower water, here we are, Christian Brothers brandy, what the doctor ordered. Man enough?"

"Lad enough for a couple of fingers," says Tink, cracking his knuckles on the sofa. "Well, Vince, it's a pyramid. But listen, should we shut windows or lower shades?"

"You cold?"

"Thinking about security."

Vince shakes his head. "The lot's vacant on this side.

The Runkles can eavesdrop on the back bedroom, so you and my granddaughter better watch yourselves, but here we're cool. Nobody on the street after nine except now and again old widow Crabbe with her Chihuahua, but they're both deaf. We can leave those poor window shades up too. They'd fall apart if we tried to pull them. Dry rot."

Tink nods, licking the rim of his snifter.

Vince catches a wrist atop his head and lifts legs onto the coffee table. "Maybe you meant some other kind of security."

Tink shakes his head. "Whatever." Mild bay air stirs silk poppies beside the television set. In the rear of the trailer a bathroom door opens on a flushing toilet.

"Spill your guts, boy, Miami this ain't. Baltimore this ain't even. I've never heard of electronic snooping here. We're not situated to pipeline drugs or assault weapons, and when it comes to sheer capital, if you had it would you choose Manatee for your declining years? I'm not complaining but sometimes we have to be realistic. So shoot. A pyramid, you say. Egyptian? Aztec? Seeing-eye like on a buck? Glass one to concentrate energy of the universe? An orgone pyramid maybe?"

"Financial," Tink explains. "See, we were thinking."

Vince's eyes barely flicker.

Tink nods. "You understand how it works, right? One day you get a fax or a letter that says to transfer funds to the top destination on the list, which you then erase and add your own at the bottom. Say it's a list of ten." Tink sets the snifter on the floor. "Then you fax ten copies to friends or acquaintances with money to burn, giving them the same instructions. Maybe it goes to their accountants or lawyers, business managers. Two or three of the ten may be pussies but the rest are sports and, who knows, one or two may really be against a wall. Maybe they got a positive on an OIDS test. Maybe they have a habit that's done a quantum flip.

"So then you wait and watch. What can I say?—arithmetic does it for you. We worked it out with a tree diagram. If only seven out of each ten keep the faith you'll receive three hundred million times your original investment. Say that was a hundred, you get thirty billion, rounded off."

"You sure make it sound good, Tink."

"That's part of the point, isn't it?"

Vince lets his hands fall and flop onto the sofa. "I once got a numbers courier for a fare, before governments started taking over the racket. We spent half a day stopping at shoeshine shops and bars. Little Sicilian, weaselly, couldn't stop talking. He told me about one of these schemes. He'd lost a couple hundred, which was money then.

"He lost the first century playing by the rules, but the chain petered out before his name moved more than a notch or two. So then, would you believe, it comes by him again. This time he puts down his second C and sends out the list with his name on top. Trouble is, everybody he sends it to realizes they can play the same game, and without the original down.

"You'd need a damn good story, Tink, to talk me into playing along, human nature being what it is. Plus, the arrangement is illegal. Where will my great-grandchildren come from if you're in one prison and Neesy's in another? Want some biscotti with that brandy? I'd say you need to start again at square one."

Tink waves his hands. "Details. Plus you're shitting me about your numbers runner. The mob wouldn't have used a fucking taxi for collections. They must've had their own armored cars even then."

"Not for Brooklyn Italian grannies' pennies. Plus the Sicilian's hearse was in the shop."

"Okay, maybe, Vince. We get to know each other better and I'll read you better. But Christ, if only one in ten bellies up at each level you've still got unbelievable return, and the odds can be better. See, the way I look at it is this. Down in the end of the eastern corridor, talking Lauderdale to Key West, there's so much capital backed up they'll be happy to play with some of it. And then as far as compliance, those dudes can more or less guarantee that everybody plays by the rules.

"Vince, baby, listen to Tink. Neesy and me aim to set it up in Key West. It works, cool. If not, we've still had fun trying. And old Neese and I were talking before dinner, and what I'm authorized to say is, we'd more than like for you to join us for the ride down."

Lillian Margiotta should be asleep in her Murphy bedlet. Instead she risks sitting in the light of the full moon, on a needlepoint footstool, embroidered satin sleeves drooping over her knees to the carpet, black and silver hair unwound.

Lillian has no use for old wives' tales about moonlight making you loony, nor does she suppose there's any danger of her growing fangs and claws. Between gatherings of point d'esprit she watches something bright and nearly invisible twinkle past the moon. Maybe a communication or spy satellite, maybe a commercial prison ship, or are they all in the water? Maybe a Star Wars base put up by a television president, maybe the president in the pet cemetery.

But isn't the full moon supposed to do something else, something more serious? Maybe if it catches you thinking about your true love, and only when you're asleep and dreaming of him.

So Vince wants some nighttime company, so what else is new? Lillian wiggles a slipper, its velvet and silk gone black and white in the moonlight, and dislodges a moth. Vince's weewee wants company, that's for sure. His pokes got tolerable and sometimes agreeable after the girls' birth, and the little she heard from other wives made her tally his ardor as a qualified plus, if hardly essential. The one time Lillian was unfaithful, age forty-eight so it could only have been an accident, when it was happening it was like nothing was happening, and that thirty-year-old hadn't lacked for ardor. In more recent decades, though, none of it's been much more than tolerable, and Lillian has had to wean Vince some.

Oh but he always got his pokes elsewhere. Authorities allow as how men reach sexual peaks at twenty-two or so and then decline, while women don't even start to level off until menopause. That's one rule the Margiottas have run counter to. Some biological timer in Vince seems to have gone haywire back in the dark ages and broken some governor. His interest hasn't dipped for even as much as a month, not even with that lingering pneumonia for Christ's sake he caught celebrating his sixtieth birthday in the rain. "You want to wear black for a reason?" the doctor said. "Keep Vince up here in this bad air and cold for another winter or two." That very evening Lillian made up her mind, on her back looking up at the scandal of a half-dead husband's ghastly face, into his rheumy eyes, dodging drool as he worked into her and out, she made up her mind. When finally he lay beside her wheezing with a voiceless rattle Lillian said, "It's time for us to move to Florida, Vince. We've entered our waning years."

But sex has never meant much to Lillian and if truth be told she has never submitted more than she really wanted to, so if now she telephoned him and said, "I'll come back, but no more pokes period," she knows he'd be crestfallen but still relieved.

No, sex isn't what put Lillian in this dwarf trailer, where she may love her scarecrow but she's not exactly honoring him and certainly not obeying. What put Lillian here and keeps her here feels more like the rising gorge that twenty years ago, after a good number of clear silences and other epistolary expressions of impatience to a whining sister in Utica, made Lillian just not even open the handful of letters that followed, or the two or three Christmas and birthday cards, and return the receiver to its cradle the time Stella tried to call.

Lillian's impatience with Vince is for a hundred things, pickles he's never let her buy, his snoring, and maybe most of all for his body's relentless aging before her very eyes. His ears, for instance, Lillian could talk an hour about how Vince's ears have grown and thinned and drooped and changed color and sprouted hair, and the hair thickened and whitened. If you live with somebody you're not supposed to notice such gradual changes, so how come Lillian does? Because Vince acts like nothing has changed?

"You're dying, buster," she's felt like telling him, throwing it in his face. What would he say?

Lillian sniffs and shakes her head. The truth is probably even stranger. Unfortunately the truth of the matter may not even have all that much to do with Vince. Maybe the truth is, Lillian wants to pay attention to herself now in the time remaining. Because the end will come, and when it comes with its awful smell of baling wire, it'll be all the same if Vince is there holding her hand or not.

Lillian stands and stretches. No need to worry about the remains, either. If Vince still wants the corpses to go into the Jersey plot, fine, if not, fine.

Before dawn Vola Byrd casts parsley seed in the full moon naked as a jay (except for galoshes and the poke flapping on her hip), the way she saw her parents and neighbors do it, in Oklahoma cornfields in her childhood. Some said sowing at night gave the corn an affinity with the sowers and with the harvesters to come, since people planted their own seed at night. Some said doing it naked (as people then seldom did with their own seed) gave the corn a candor and a propulsion. Some Okies said corn sown at night would sprout "sleepless" stalks that grew round the clock. You did it when the whole moon was in the sky, some said, because it gave the seed a better start, because it had more to look up to. Or the light tricked the seed into taking even night for day. It might work with parsley too, no harm in trying.

Glumma glumma. White as a sheet Vola Byrd late of storied reaches of Manhattan-area real estate tramps in rattling galoshes over turned clods behind a caboose near a west Florida freeway that still purrs. Seed slides off her cold hand into the mild air.

TWO

Miami, Key West, Gunga-Munga, Manatee, the Everglades

Manatee, Manatee Springs, and East Manatee slip away behind the orange coupe. It slows, as if doubtful of the southbound freeway's low haze, and then hops on. Denise Passaro at the wheel sports silver wraparound shades, a Florida pink ruched halter, and matching patio pajamas. Yesterday afternoon, while Gramps was out paying respects to one lady or another, Neesy and Tink rocked Gramps's trailer on its foundations. Remembering as she drives, Denise entertains the possibility of a glowing future for the two of them. She lets pass a decommissioned prison van of whackos before she blows Tink a quick kiss.

Tink reciprocates, noodling on a ukulele, riding sideways with his back against the door so he can face all three other voyagers. Over his headrest he says, "So Lillian wouldn't buy a visit to the Keys? What's with her, no sense of adventure?"

Vince snorts and caws, waving away imaginary smoke or midges. "I . . ."

"Bummersville," Tink continues. "I mean, some couples find stimulation in a mere new set of sights. Huh, babe." He leans over to elbow Denise.

Beside Vince in the back seat Vola Byrd says, "Hmm." She glances this way and that. "I didn't notice a rumble seat on this buggy."

"No." Denise shakes her head.

"No," sputters Vince. "No, I knew she wouldn't come. That's why I did her the courtesy of inviting her."

"Er," says Tink, "I was joking. I didn't actually think you'd asked her, man."

Vola laughs. "I wonder what would have happened if she'd accepted." She settles back and hums.

Blinking lights whiz along the freeway, palm fronds and hibiscus, egrets and ruined haciendas and blue electronic jungles. The light bunchy traffic seems benign until the Caloosahatchee bridge when, what's that fishtailing between lanes up ahead? Better ease over into the breakdown, Denise. Looks like a drug convoy with hypersteroided goons fore and aft. Denise lets them disappear into the depths of Fort Myers before she slips back into the southbound stream. "Well done, kid," says Tink.

Miami, Key West, Gunga-Munga, Manatee, the Everglades

Shortly the route veers east onto the Tamiami Trail, through swamp and marshland across the southern end of the state. "My, my," says Vola, "a soul could get lost back in here. What are those trees, and is that Spanish moss, that looks like cobwebs?"

"Sure is," says Vince. "And the trees are what this part of the swamp is named for, Big Cypress."

"Baltimore this ain't," says Tink.

"Really," says Neesy. "Although a body could get lost in parts of Baltimore too."

"I'll say this," says Vola, "this must be the most unimproved territory I've set foot in. Well, not exactly foot."

"Tire," offers Tink.

"Whatever. Compared to this, my childhood Oklahoma was Versailles. Hey, a For Sale sign?" Askew and blistered on a sand hill cresting the muck. "I thought this was federal park."

Vince hawks. "Unfinished. It's trying to be a park, but they don't have the right laws in place. You wouldn't believe it to look at it, but people all over the world own dribs and drabs of the Big Cypress."

"We read about it," says Denise. "Land fever. People bought without coming for a walk around. A wade around, it would have been. That sign must be a relic, though, because didn't we read that only the federal government can buy here now?"

"I'm starting to remember," says Vola. "Fifty, sixty years ago, a bubble. Mostly small investors left holding the bag. Not my sort of real estate."

"Still," observes Tink, "some principles must be the same. Buy low, sell high."

Vola sighs. "Tell me about it. Oh well, easy come, easy go. Say, what's that with an American flag over it?"

When the convertible has tooled to a stop, the group discovers that the shed houses the Ochopee post office, smallest in the country according to the postmistress, and serving two hundred swamp families. Since it's noon and there's no telling what might lie ahead, the group picnics on the grass under the flag. The sky seems to cloud earlier in the day here than in Manatee.

On the road again, as the older passengers doze and Tink drives, Denise opens her laptop to pore over the chain letter opening.

Miami, Key West, Gunga-Munga, Manatee, the Everglades

> This letter has gone around the world nine times. It has been sent to you for good luck. You will receive fabulous money within days, provided you don't break the chain. This is no gag. This letter is causing seismic changes in the international distribution of wealth. Use your head and read on.

Is it good? The style settings seem to work okay. Denise folds down the screen and muses.

Suppose this scam makes Tink and her richer than billionaires, then what? Will it force them to marry for the tax advantage? Even then, would Tink be more likely to love her the rest of his life? On easy street, mightn't he roam quicker and farther? Mightn't Denise find herself whiling nights away with simulacra in her personal game room in her private palace with gold toilets? Small comfort if Tink didn't come home. Out cheating, like Gramps snoring in the back, with Denise cooling her heels like Lillian this very minute back in Manatee. Clunkety clunk, clunkety clunk, what? The coupe gasps and dies. "Eh?" says Vince and "Uh?" says Vola, as Tink pilots them to a halt on the shoulder. Neither Tink nor Denise succeeds in reviving their car, Vola never owned one and knows beans, and Vince explains that, with everything modular and computerized, there's no point in his even lifting the hood. There hasn't been other traffic in the past hour. The four think. A brown and olive slough stretches from the roadbed to a bank where dragonflies hover under fringes of Spanish moss, and a marsh wren moves through underbrush like a mouse. The still water dimples. Attentive nostrils and eyes surface. A bittern cries.

Denise spreads a roadmap on the hood. "The nearest town is Pinecrest on this loop road. Tink, let's you and me bicycle back there and call Triple A. We should get there in an hour, the land's flat. Meantime, you guys relax. Should you flag down somebody, maybe their emergency phone will work."

"Sounds good," says Tink. He shakes his head. "We had this buggy checked out in Baltimore." He bounces a ten-speed and then another.

"Okay," says Vola.

"Okay, then," says Vince. "Watch your step back in there."

"Don't worry, Gramps."

Miami, Key West, Gunga-Munga, Manatee, the Everglades

Tink calls over his shoulder, "You two behave yourselves."

Although the loop road needs paving, and a cloudburst forces the cyclists to shelter under a cabbage palm, still they roll into Pinecrest before three. Curs snap at their heels past the few houses and trailers, the Pinecrest and Gatorhook taverns, and the grocery, until they stop at Jim's Exxon. Jim is out catching turtles but his Lucy thinks she might be able to solve their problem. "Let me lock up, and we'll take my tow truck just in case. You'uns can lash your bikes to her. There's room in the cab for all three of us'uns."

As ancient thin Lucy coaxes her wrecker back through the village Tink remarks, "We just came from another trailer park, on the Gulf Coast. But it didn't have houses, and it was bigger."

"More law abiding too I'll allow." Lucy waves to a friend traipsing out of the Gatorhook. "Maybe more bushytailed too, but that's neither here nor there. Whoo-ee, though, used to be, you'uns show up here on a Sattidy night, you'd be lucky to get away walking. County jail's three hundred miles away by road. We had critters wouldn't come out of the swamp until they heard jigging and smelled sour mash, and they brought their heat."

"Heat?" asks Denise.

"That's right, sugar pie. Possum guns, Sattidy night specials, every kind. Not one in ten with a permit. The 'Glades is quieter now, but I still packs heat on this stretch."

"Where did you say the county jail is?" inquires Tink.

"County seat. Key West, Florida. Posse'd forget who they was after. Okay, here's the Trail. That must be you'uns's wheels up there. Don't know if I'd'a' left her unattended, but I reckon there weren't much option."

"Uh," says Tink, "she wasn't unattended."

"Where could they be?" asks Denise. All listen to the silent swamp.

"Let me toot," says Lucy.

The wrecker's blast flushes a marsh wren across the slough. It flutters a few feet and then drops back into undergrowth. Nearer, nostrils and eyes sink beneath the surface of the opaque water. On the front seat of the runabout Vola sits up, rubbing her neck. "Vince?"

In the back seat Vince sits up and stretches. "Caught me

napping. Well, well, look if those hot-dog youngsters didn't bring Triple A."

"Ain't Triple A, Mister," says Lucy leaning in the window, "but I may be able to cure what ails you howsomever." While Tink returns the bicycles to their carrier, Lucy spends a few minutes under the hood and then says, "Try her now." The engine springs to life. "Looky here," Lucy says, "nearest I can explain, she needed more air. The carburetor had got discombobulated. Now shove that wallet right back where you pulled it. You can buy me a drink at the Gatorhook if you're ever back this way." She nudges Vola with an elbow. "He looks spry, but you needn't worry. A drink's all I meant. Where you'uns headed?"

"County seat," says Denise. "We'll tell the sheriff not to lose any sleep about this end of the county."

"Shoot, I reckon they got the sheriff sweeping floors at a money laundry down there now. If I was you'uns I'd keep my eyes peeled in the Keys. Bye."

With Denise at the wheel the group sets off once again east on the Tamiami Trail. By the time they reach Greater Miami a dome of light is forming over the city, brighter than the ones over Baltimore and Tampa, and more colorful and restless with its roving searchlights. Salsa and cumbia, merengue and rap, and here reggae, hip-hop, and tango, and now calypso and junkanoo float through alleys and streets and under freeways. Since accommodations may be uncertain to the south, best pull in somewhere here for the night. The Noches Incantadas under a Bacardi billboard looks inexpensive, and the second-story rooms should be safe.

In the motel office a boy explains that all the rooms have cable, magic fingers, and deadbolts. "Good," says Vince. "You have two doubles?"

"Hold on, there, tiger," says Vola.

"Eh?"

Vola strikes a pose. "Don't get me wrong. Your conscience is your own affair, and I'm flattered by whatever designs you have, assuming it's not just your wallet talking. But I'm an old-fashioned girl who likes to make up her own mind." She turns to the bemused desk boy. "For tonight, we'll have a double and two singles."

Signing the register, Vince says, "No harm in trying. Maybe I'll get invited in for a nightcap."

"If he supplies the bottle, maybe," says Vola.

Miami, Key West, Gunga-Munga, Manatee, the Everglades

"In fact," says Vince, "where's the ice machine? You're all invited to my room for a cocktail before dinner." He scratches his head. "Speaking of which, Junior, are there any good cafeterias in walking distance? And is walking safe?"

It is and there are, and shortly the now glowing group proceeds two blocks east on the musical sidewalk, skirting bag ladies and gentlemen and steering clear of an idling stretch limo with smoked windows. Aircraft rise like bubbles in the volatile light over the city, and a stealth bomber slips into its approach corridor.

In Las Palmas Cafeteria, when Vince asks a server to season Vola's pork with Spanish fly, the man shakes his head and says, "No English." It sounds like an order but it's probably mere information, for no one here seems to speak English. Still, you can choose by pointing and pay in dollars and, all things considered, Las Palmas resembles Neptune's in Manatee enough for the group to depart well satisfied.

Automobiles of many sorts prowl streets where laughing pedestrians deal and flirt in clicking Spanish overlaid with English and Vietnamese, and homeless bunk against storefront walls and in alleyways. Lights and objects of every color shower and bloom in the sky. "Botanica," says a sign over an open doorway.

"Let's have a look," says Tink.

"I suppose it's safe," says Vola.

The fragrant hole-in-the-wall displays merchandise on shelves and card tables, and behind glass at the cash register, where a boy who could be the twin of the motel clerk offers a restrained hello. At the back a beaded curtain gives onto what seems a smaller room where two seated women speak in undertones, in Spanish, the younger one's palm open on the older one's lap.

But what merchandise is this? Statuettes and paintings of crucifixes, saints, Indian chiefs, and dictators mingle with inscribed candles, salves, and strings and pots of beads, and rows of jars on the back wall hold doubtful organic matter suspended in varicolored liquids. "Say," Vince tells the boy, "my Spanish has got rusty. What does that Botanica over your door mean? Sounds like an encyclopedia."

"Or vice versa," says the boy without a smile. "It means this kind of store. You wish to make purchases?"

"We're tourists," Denise explains. "I hope you'll forgive our curiosity. We may only be window-shopping."

Miami, Key West, Gunga-Munga, Manatee, the Everglades

"Wait a sec," says Tink. "This is one of those Santeria stores, isn't it? Denise, remember I told you how me and Snake and Bobo hid out in one in east Baltimore during a riot? That one was half barbershop. I don't remember if it said Botanica."

"What's Santeria?" asks Vola.

Tink turns to the clerk. "Maybe you can explain better than me."

"Maybe," says the boy. "It's like a religion, the part that gets things done at least. The business end, you might say. A botanica sells supplies. Slaves developed Santeria out of their own religions and their Spanish masters' Catholicism."

"Voodoo?" asks Vola.

"That's more in the islands. Santeria's with us here."

"Who's 'us'?" asks Vince.

The boy shrugs. "Santeros. Most of us are Latinos."

"So you're in Baltimore too," says Denise.

"Every major city, and all over the Spanish Sunbelt and up both coasts. Parts of Canada."

"But listen," says Vince, "how come I never heard of you? Do you have churches and priests? I wonder if the Pope knows about you."

"Could be. As for you, you must not have traveled with the right crowd. We don't have churches, the kind you mean, but we do have priests. In Santeria, the highest priest is the Babalaw."

In her reedy voice, Vola tries out the word. "Babalaw. So is it a kind of pope?"

"You could say so, about a good Babalaw. Some say a good one gets more done for ordinary people than the pope can. Some say a good one's power is limitless."

"Oh," says Denise. "You have more than one, then."

"A hundred in Florida alone."

"Hang on," says Tink. "Didn't what's-his-face, Lucille Ball's husband, have a song about Babalaws?"

"Babaloo," says Vola. "Desi Arnaz. Is he still kicking?"

Vince says, "He checked out years ago. I thought it was Boogaloo, though. But listen, pal, what qualifications do these Babalaws need? Is there a college of cardinals for electing new ones?"

"A sign shows potential. A mark, a vision, whatever. The apprentice studies with a master until it's time to be initiated."

Vola says, "You make it sound simple. I was wondering,

though, just what powers these Babalaws are supposed to have."

"'Supposed'?" asks the boy.

"What kind are they said to have?"

"Kinds called magic, knowing the future, and so forth. If you're worried about what's going to happen or if you want to make something happen, you see your Babalaw. Say you want somebody to love you or come back to you, or you want money, or you don't want to die right away."

"Holy shit," says Tink. "Florida's something else. Suppose we wanted to have a look at one of these dudes. Where might we find one?"

The boy almost smiles. "You're looking at one."

"You?" says Denise. "You can't be over eighteen. How long have you been one?"

"Two years. Most are older, it's true."

"What was your initiation like? Or is it secret?"

"Part is. You don't want to know any of it, though."

"Okay," says Tink. "But, could you use your magic for us?" He chuckles uncertainly.

"I wouldn't, unless you became my godchildren."

"How long would that take?"

"Too long for you."

Like a fretful child Denise pushes black ringlets away from her eyebrows and says, "Don't you ever help strangers?"

A moment passes. The boy says, "Yes."

Another moment. The boy slides a jeweler's tray out of the display case and sets it on the counter. Across midnight velvet lies a grid of little objects, natural and manufactured, twinkling, gleaming, and dull, seashell, golf tee, pebble, cuttlebone, penny, quartz crystal. "Charms," says Denise.

"Yes. For thirty dollars you may take one with you."

"How about a century for four?" says Tink.

"Century?"

"Hundred smackers. Seems you ought to cut us a group rate."

"Ah." The boy pauses. "In truth, I think this is the only one who should buy one." He touches Vince's near arm through crinkled seersucker.

"More unexpected demands on your wallet there, Tiger," says Vola.

"Why me?" Vince asks the ceiling as he lays bills on the counter. "*Why* me?" he asks the boy.

"Good question. Why not, though? Now look, the best way to choose is to pass your hand over the tray slowly, like divining. You'll know when you cross what's right for you."

Vince closes his eyes. In the back room the two women who have been talking stop. As through a crevice in air Vince's hand inches over the tray. The boy clears his throat and Vince's hand freezes, and now descends and closes. It rises, swivels, and opens.

"What we got there?" asks Tink.

On the bluish palm lies a tiny car. Denise sets it upright. It seems to be zinc with traces of yellow paint and isinglass at its windows. "What must I do?" asks Vince.

"Keep it with you on a key ring or whatever, or like a piece of change. You don't have to talk to it or anything."

"What will it do?"

"It's for protection, and to help wishes come true. Specific guarantees can backfire so I don't make them, but I will guarantee this: it will do all it can."

Vince drops the car into his pocket. "We're headed into the Keys. Maybe I'll need this down there. Okay, gang, shall we get some shut-eye? Thanks again, kid."

"Right," says Tink. "Nice botanica you got here."

Vola nods and smiles.

"Bye now, Babalaw," says Denise.

At Las Noches Incantadas Denise and Tink enjoy magic fingers and each other before a hologram video wall running steam scan through the multi-X channels. Vola also, having pleaded headache to beg off nightcaps or more, tries the motel video. She spends a peaceful half hour with the Gideon channel before sleep. In his room Vince, having urged drinks only perfunctorily, opens drapes a touch so that he can glance up at beautiful garish sky over a dangerous city, as he sits writing.

"Dear Lillian, What are you doing this very? I wonder if this letter will reach you. I wonder does the postal service deliver anything but junk any more. It's been years since either of us had a real letter. Does that toy trailer of yours even have a box? But I didn't feel like phoning tonight or faxing, with my heart full of tears.

"What will you be doing when you read this if you do? You still let us talk, so I don't think you should burn this letter without reading it.

"Here's an idea. This trip shouldn't last long, and if you want me to come back before it's over, say the word. We're in Miami and tomorrow we shoot for Key West. Our granddaughter's setting herself up for heartbreak with her blarney slinger, I fear, but that's down the road, and they're not bad company. Neither is this Vola Byrd, even though she's drawing the line at hanky-pank, believe it or not, and still letting me foot her bills.

"But Lil, my idea for you is, since you've got me out of your hair for a while, you can think more clearly about what's keeping you from coming back to me. Maybe talk it over with somebody, even Gwen Runkle might help you get clear so you can tell me what I have to do. I will do anything.

"By the time I'm in Manatee again maybe you'll know how we can live back together, and tell me.

"Carissima, if you don't, what's going to happen to us?"

In a large clear fresh south Florida winter morning that seems to have raised its eyebrows the four bid Las Noches adios and drive to an older section of the city for a New-York-style deli breakfast at Wolfie's. With a parcel of the restaurant's half-sour pickles for later they stroll, beside a park whose residents have begun stirring, back to the orange coupe.

* * *

Part Two

As Gwen and Brent Runkle have done for the past twelve years, they don mourning on the first of February and wear it for the week following. Day after day they mourn, Gwen in powdery black shifts and under ashen veils, Brent in lustrous black slacks and polos or at the pool in a black racing suit. Most of Manatee knows the cause and forgoes any but the most pitying and indirect allusions whenever the Runkles venture forth from their doublewide. The Runkles venture forth seldom during the week, Brent for laps, Gwen to drop off new clocks at the craft fair, the two for a quiet dinner at Neptune's.

At home the laser reads Albinoni out the sound system, as the Runkles drift from room to room, past cold cuts and cookies spread in the dining room, drawn drapes in the parlor, silent drills and dimmed lights in the hobby center. At night too the Runkles mourn, in black silk mail-order nightwear and bedclothes. On the morning of the seventh, their estranged daughter's birthday, neither moves nor speaks after they awaken, until Brent sighs.

Almost imperceptibly, Gwen nods. Brent understands and slides over to plant a kiss on her moist cheek. "Yes," he whispers into her ear, "we don't deserve this cross. If only we could turn back the hands of time. All the same, we have each other, and that's more than we could say for lots." When Gwen seems to nod again with closed eyes, Brent continues. "We've always been troupers. What's past is past, dear."

Gwen slides toward the headboard and sits up. "Brentie dear, today, even today, is the first day of the rest of our lives together. That's much to be thankful for."

"More than much." Brent sits up too.

Gwen's head trembles. "I have a proposition to make. Dear, I propose that we decrease our mourning a day a year, for the next seven. After all," she squeezes Brent's hand, "this is the twenty-first century, and there has to be a statute of limitations."

"You're probably right."

Gwen clasps her hands under her chin. "And I was thinking. A better way to mourn might be to comfort those less fortunate. This afternoon, I think I'll slip over to Lillian Margiotta's trailerette to commiserate about the breakup of her marriage. It should do us both good." Gwen's gaze wheels to the window striped with blue dawn. "Although, just between us, I think she might be lucky to be rid of that buzzard. What a relief to have him out of our neighborhood!"

"I wouldn't exactly call old Vince a buzzard, Gwen. Although I know what you mean."

The Runkles retire to respective bathrooms and then meet in the breakfast nook. With juice they spin a sundial lazy Susan for vitamins and a BC for Gwen's arthritis. Each settles down with a section of the *Manatee Mercury*. As Brent leans over the sports section, sightlines run from Gwen's eyes through coffee steam to a spot behind her hubby's right ear, a well-defined blue spot she does not recall noticing before.

OIDS? The disease does manifest itself so. What are other early symptoms? Fatigue, no? Weakness, GI distress, and aren't there queerer ones too, a stammer?

Never having known a victim, Gwen has never had call to learn about the diagnosis. Surely not here, though. There haven't been any cases in Manatee. A few have been reported in Miami, even Tampa, and apparently it's reaching epidemic proportions in Key West, but surely not here. Furthermore Brent can't have been out of Gwen's more or less immediate company, except for his laps, more than the odd hour since retirement. Nor can he be much of a sexual adventurer. Are there non-venereal vectors?

Of course you do expect dermal irregularity in the aging. If Gwen has maintained an even milkiness over the years, Brent like Manatee's other residents hosts an ever-increasing array of growths and splotches. Best not alarm him then, best just keep a weather eye out.

Brent looks up. "Gent around the corner, Smith, won last week's horseshoe pitch-off. Tai Chi membership's up. Know what I was just thinking? This rag ought to have a crafts page. At least a column. Let's speak with the editor."

The Runkles moon through the morning in the doublewide and its grounds. After a late lunch in the gazebo followed by naps, while Brent heads for the pool Gwen drives to where Lillian Margiotta's trailer is supposed to be. Where it in fact is, although it takes repeated passes to find. Gwen parks under a fire tree. On the stoop she rings the doorbell. Hearing nothing, she knocks.

Lillian Margiotta lays aside Vince's letter. Wonder is he trying his carissimas on the floozie with him? May they do him some good. As for Lillian, she's always been proof against lovebird talk. "What are 'we' going to do now?" Lillian would answer if he were here. "We'll do what we choose, if we can. Give me a break." Lillian slides back her chair and steps to the door and opens it on Gwen Runkle.

Gwen bends forward, hands clasped on her breast. "Lillian, dear, I was in the neighborhood and thought I should see how you were holding up. Brent and I haven't lost hope for you, you know, and this moment of our own bereavement lends yours an added poignancy. It occurred to me to do a little snooping, and I've learned that we have a marriage counselor right here in Manatee, specializing in the maturer union. You don't look nearly so bad as I expected, though. You must be keeping a stiff upper lip."

"I'd ask you in for tea, Gwen," says Lillian, "except I have a headache."

"Of course. Brent and I want to entice you out of your seclusion soon. Perhaps you'll join us for a dinner at Neptune's, almost like old times. Or you might venture back to the old neighborhood for a cocktail with us. Brent's old-fashioneds have improved since the last time you and Vince sampled them."

"Yes, let's do something. I'd enjoy it."

"I'm sure you would. Of course you know Vince has

flown his coop with your granddaughter and her friend. Which reminds me, there's something you really ought to know, even though it causes you pain. Brace yourself, dear. Vince took someone else along for the trip. The Byrd woman from New York who's been squatting in the caboose. I was bound to tell you, Lillian. Of course everyone knows Vince has hardly been a model of faithfulness, but this seems a different order of magnitude."

Lillian nods. "Thanks, Gwen. You're thoughtful. I can't say I'm surprised, though. And now I really must nurse this headache and let you get on about your business. Ciao." She shuts the door. Listening to Gwen's car pull away, Lillian crumples the Noches Incantadas envelope and flips it into a wastebasket. She lifts the letter and hesitates. The first from him in . . . how many years? Fluttering a corner with her finger, she feels almost young.

Lillian shrugs. "I'm not young, I'm on death's doorstep, as sure as that nosy Parker was just on mine, that goody two-shoes. Death's doorstep." All the same, Lillian doesn't crumple the letter. She opens a cedar box of loose photographs and slips the folded letter in among them.

* * *

Part Two

Having spent their first Key West night in an airport motel, the Baltimore-Manatee quartet has moved to Murtry's Trailer Court in the heart of the Old Town. Hidden behind bamboo and flowering bougainvillea, and shaded by flowering poinciana and frangipani, the court occupies half a city block. Vola with her realtor's nose has learned that an earlier building on the site housed a cigar factory and then a body shop, and then stood empty until fifteen years ago when the Murtry family razed it to build a luxe bed-and-breakfast, but unwise investments and an ailing patriarch derailed that plan. The deceased patriarch's descendants have grown too quarrelsome and litigious to pay much attention to feelers from potential buyers, so that the valuable land has since underlain only a cinderblock office and a semicircle of seedy Airstreams.

The seediness attracted Vince and when rates proved commensurate, and it turned out that sitting rooms with Castro Convertible sofas could double as bedrooms, he persuaded Vola to share a trailer. The quartet has taken two Airstreams for a week. Most other occupants seem tourists although the Korean family and the black and white gay alcoholics look resident.

Miami, Key West, Gunga-Munga, Manatee, the Everglades

After a day of boating and snorkeling among farther islands, and a day spent learning Key West topography and history aboard the Waterfront RR, a line of open trolley cars pulled by a miniature black locomotive engine with a smokestack and cowcatcher, on the morning of the third day the group breakfasts in the old Cubanita off Duval Street, the main shopping thoroughfare in the Old Town.

Besides a reserved Japanese couple, all the other customers enjoying cafe con leche and Cuban bread with sausage and eggs in the busy little restaurant resemble Ernest Hemingway. One at the next table explains that he and his companions have come from North America, Australia, and Europe to compete in the Hemingway Lookalike contest, a traditional high point of Papa Week, which begins today and will include scholarly conferences, displays of memorabilia, and write-offs. "The Lookalike contest is tomorrow at two in the San Carlos. I was fourth runner-up last year," the grizzled man offers before turning back to his grizzled companions.

"I thought they looked familiar," Tink tells his tablemates. "I must have seen this Hemingway on Letterman. Or does he host one of those Etosha shows?"

"Isn't he dead?" says Vola. "He wrote books. My, this coffee is fabulous." From her floppy sea-grass basket she extracts a chromed thermos bottle and waves over a pretty Cuban-American waitress. "Sugar, could you fill this with that delicious cafe con leche for me?"

Vince has been thinking. "I think Hemingway must have checked out before you were born, Tink. So this Lookalike contest must be, what would you say, retroactive. But he did live here. You must have been billing and cooing with my granddaughter yesterday on the trolley when we passed his house."

"More likely we were brainstorming," says Tink. "We have the deal fine-tuned now, so today we'll split off from you folks. Make hay while the sun shines."

"What's the first step?" Vola asks.

"Locate high rollers," explains Denise.

"How?"

She shrugs. "Serendipity? You tell us. The people we're looking for have money to burn but it's ill-gotten gains, so we might as likely find them in those shacks over by the fort as in a Casa Marina penthouse. We'll have to play it by ear. What are your plans?"

Miami, Key West, Gunga-Munga, Manatee, the Everglades

Vola lowers the thermos into her basket. "I'm in the mood for window-shopping."

Vince slips some bills out of his wallet and presses them into Vola's hand. "Don't leave it all in the windows. You deserve some treats."

Vola sighs. Denise drops a handkerchief and she and Tink tactfully search under the table for it. Vola says, "I would enjoy picking up a trinket or two, Vince, but I want you to understand, I won't necessarily be forking over any quid pro quo. A girl has to be careful about accepting gifts. Want your money back?"

Vince shakes his head and knocks on the table with his knife handle. "You kids can come up for air now, we've negotiated the minefield. Keep the money, Vola, and my admiration too—you've held out longer than any female in living memory."

"What's your agenda, Gramps?"

Vince yawns. "Think I'll stroll around and pretend it's the distant past. I've wrapped up my world tour with a good month solacing Bermuda wahines, and a spicy Havana week. I'm here to catch the train for Penn Station. The world is young."

The foursome scoots back chairs and files out. At the cash register Tink rests an elbow on the counter, chews a toothpick, and tells Vince, "After that action I guess you won't look for any more while you stroll."

"Probably not," says Vince. "On the other hand, I wouldn't want to get rusty. Everything should be in good working order if Vola finally decides to be merciful."

As Vola clucks, Denise says, "Don't forget, Gramps, this place is crawling with OIDS. This morning when I went out for the paper, they were moving somebody out of the old commissary on a stretcher. He looked like a mummy, and he had the blue spots. You can get it from anybody and it's not worth taking a chance. The only sex that's safe is safe sex. I saw a condom boutique around the corner."

"Don't worry your pretty little head. I always have a safe or two in my wallet. Anyway the incubation's long enough for me to be effectively immune. Plus now I have the Babalaw car to protect me. Vola, shall we leave lunch open? I may sneak back to the trailer for a nap."

"Sure thing, Tiger," says Vola. "Maybe he's telling me to stay away so he can have an assignation? No, but if he's napping I wouldn't want to wake him. Say, Neesy, why don't you give me your key in case I need a nap. You two won't be back before five, will you?" Vola drops the key into her basket. As Denise and Tink pedal away she calls, "You kids be careful."

Vince walks Vola to Duval. Gulls wheel and cry in the clear morning. From the facade of the restored San Carlos Opera House flutter silken flags, and across adjoining storefronts stir pennants, posters, and balloons. Cyclists weave arabesques through the line of creeping automotive traffic in the narrow street, sidewalks throng with natives and tourists, and English and other languages ride like flotsam on a tide of Spanish.

Vince says, "Don't get lost. And remember my granddaughter's caution. Women are at risk too. Look there." Across Duval in a sunny alcove a blue-spotted woman no older than forty begs alms with the malady's characteristic twitch.

After a moment Vola says, "In Manhattan they had them out of sight by that time." She sighs. "Ta-ta."

Gaunt Vince watches gangly Vola disappear into the crowd and then he wanders down quiet side streets. In luminous shade under ficus and palms leaning over stucco walls and cactus and pink, yellow, and red hibiscus, he passes trellises and peeling gingerbread, sawgrass, yellow thryallis and allamanda, purple oleander, tangerine ixora and heliconia, stiff bird-of-paradise blooms, strings of Christmas lights, hovering dragonflies, sky-blue porch ceilings, and a wall made of bottles. He sees few people and hears no voices except when an infant laughs in an airy bedroom above, and when a woman sings a muffled "Comparsita" on a radio on a table in an empty garden.

Vince strolls through musk and jasmine, past a stone fountain tinkling in the green air, a cream-colored Silver Wraith parked under swags of peach and lavender bougainvillea, until rounding a corner he comes upon a bus disgorging tourists at the Hemingway house. He now recalls magazine photos of this Hemingway, with Ava Gardner and with a dead elephant and a marlin. What kind of books did he write, sports books, war books? *War and Peace*? Maybe it would be interesting to have a look inside the house. After the busload have disappeared Vince follows them through the gateway.

"Ten dollars," says an aged person whose gender is momentarily indeterminate, with mascara and seeming pajamas. "You like my pussy?" he says, stroking a cat in his lap. "Inside you'll see more. Fifty-odd live here, descendants of Hemingway's cats. Most have six toes like Venus. See?" He lifts one of Venus's paws. "This is a National Historic Landmark, and the money goes for upkeep. Feel free to donate more. Because of the international Hemingway industry, we have tighter security than any other Historic Landmark outside D.C. The house was built by a wealthy merchant, Asa Tift. The Hemingways bought it in 1935. You'll see Hemingway's writing study on the second floor of the pool house. He had a catwalk—catch that?—leading from his bedroom across to the study, so if inspiration struck in the middle of the night he could walk straight over. He liked to write longhand standing, so he had a special desk for that, but he also had a typing table. Nobody had computers then. His wife installed the first swimming pool in the Keys. She was trying to keep Ernest home. He had a penchant for nipping over to Cuba or Africa. There's a souvenir shop on the right as you exit. You'll find his writings electronically compacted, writings of his friends and associates, F. Scott Fitzgerald, Sinclair Lewis, Gertrude Stein, videos and holographic simulacra, and other memorabilia."

"Wait," interrupts Vince. "Did he write about Marilyn Monroe? Or marry her?"

"He wasn't married to her but he may have limned her. Ask an attendant. As I was saying, this was once the only house on the island with a second-story bath. There was no municipal running water at that time so the Hemingways had to collect rainwater or use well water. They were fortunate to have a well on the property. Mr. Hemingway enjoyed his baths, and of course nobody had air conditioning back then. Be still, Venus."

Vince quickly says, "Thanks for the info, pal."

"Keep this stub. We close for lunch in an hour but this will let you re-enter after two. Just so you know."

Vince circles the handsome house. Here are banyans, palms, and banana trees with bunches of orchids hanging from them. Sure enough, many cats chase each other and doze in the sun, and many sorts of people, among them proprietary-looking Hemingway Lookalikes, admire the vegetation and architecture. On the narrow stair to the study even thin Vince must squeeze against the stucco to let pass a pair of descending . . . Poles? Serbians? Something moves on the wall, a lizard.

Miami, Key West, Gunga-Munga, Manatee, the Everglades

Behind velvet rope the study looks inviting with its daybed and picturesque black mechanical typewriter. "I maintain," says a severe woman in sunglasses to her companions farther down the rope, "that post-ideologists betray a fatal lack of rigor. 'That's the point,' they might argue; however, any number of stinging ripostes spring to mind. I daresay some will be discomfited by what I intend to do this afternoon with *For Whom the Bell Tolls*. That session is at the hotel, by the way, not the Community College. I see my paper as a preemptive strike." She and her companions wear nametags, and one pipe-smoker with muttonchops wears a Hemingway sweatshirt.

In the entryway to the main house an array of framed drawings, black-and-white photographs, and pages of typescript with penciled revisions catches Vince's eye. Some of the photographs are of Hemingway's friends—in a Picasso painting the Gertrude Stein mentioned by the doorkeeper, one Adriana Ivancich who could almost be Lillian fifty years ago, resting her arms on the polished top of a car, Dietrich smoking, Ava Gardner vamping, and assorted men including a young Fidel Castro—but most are of Hemingway himself, young and handsome, and then through the years gaining weight and looking away from the camera as his beard grows and whitens.

Inside some tourists clump about guides who, perhaps because this is Key West's Papa Week, speak with great vivacity. Other tourists walk separately with pamphlets and headphones, and many explore on their own, conversing and commenting. Vince learns a good deal from what he overhears as he strolls the hallways and leans over more velvet rope to inspect roomy sparsely furnished rooms.

Preparation is under way for tribute and reassessment during the tenth anniversary of the centenary of the writer's birth. By dint of sheer capital the Aramco Hemingway Institute threatens to outrank either U.S. one. The game of taking potshots at the writer's sexism has fallen out of favor in all but the least prestigious reaches of the academy. Now cynical schoolchildren play the game. Directors' cuts of the old movies have come online in colorized holographic versions with remastered sound.

Surveillance cameras scan the rooms, probably to guard more against vandalism than terrorism. Vince tips an imaginary hat to one watching from the ceiling fan in the sunken bathroom. As a six-toed tabby pushes against his ankle and trips down into the room and across the brown and orange tiles, bells chime and an electronic voice announces that the house proper is closing for lunch although the souvenir and gift shop will remain open.

The busload and most other tourists leave the grounds, but Vince with a few others steps into the glass-roofed shop, to dawdle over postcards, mugs, jewelry, still and moving holograms. In one corner a life-size Hemingway shadow-boxes, and on the counter miniature Hemingways display marlins, make love, raise shotguns to their foreheads. At the exit a life-size Gertrude Stein in the Picasso pose surveys the scene and then hoists her bulk and walks away.

Cashier module scanners announce fund transfers in cardholders' preferred languages, so that here too Spanish prevails. It occurs to Vince that a good percentage of the electronic capital flowing into the souvenir shop's account must derive from the same illegal drug trade his granddaughter and her Irish beau are trying to tap. Maybe tomorrow they should flog their letter here. Vola, with her realty acumen, might enjoy a visit too.

Vince ambles onto the sidewalk. It must be twelve-thirty,

but he's not hungry. Better let the Duval Street eateries thin out some. Here's a little public garden, deserted probably because of the lunch hour, with benches that don't look uncomfortable. Lizards on the one Vince approaches twinkle out of sight.

As he is about to sit, the trunk of the adjacent tree makes a loud thwock. How's that? Vince leans to read the label, "Gumbo-limbo, *Bursera simaruba*." Thwock, thwock, from the trunk just above his head, and a sudden fragrance of resin. Gumbo-limbo? Wait, those holes in the bark . . . thwoonk, in the bench behind him, and now there, against the metal support, at the end of a fresh track ploughed in the wood, what appears to be a bullet.

Vince whirls. Under a trellised arch stands the Gertrude Stein from the souvenir shop, same brown dress and black monk's robe, cropped hair and thoughtful face. But what is she doing with her hands? Raised in front of her, the left holds a purse and steadies the right, which seems to be pointing an old-fashioned microphone toward him over the purse. Should he speak? Wait, that's no microphone, that's a fucking silencer. "Hey!" shouts Vince. Thwock, now near enough to tickle hairs on his neck. This can't be happening.

Miami, Key West, Gunga-Munga, Manatee, the Everglades

* * *

The problem, Vola thinks as she paddles through resort wear in an uncluttered shop that smells new and clean, the problem is that when Vince pressed what turned out to be five hundreds of mad money into her hand at breakfast neither of them raised the question of how long it was meant to last. Surely not the whole rest of the week, and yet as a day's allowance, was this setting a standard either of them would really want to maintain for five more days? Oh well, it's only money. Easy come, easy go.

These Scandinavian candy-colored middies would become Vola, and it would be a pleasure to try something on, take it home, spread the tissue paper and try it on again, as in the old days. In present circumstances, though, it seems wiser to dress from one of the thrifts listed in the phone book. Come to think of it, a resort Salvation Army might have nice surprises. Smaller items however like these fluorescent bangles—Vola glances at the salesgirls nattering in the back, the nearest other customer an aisle away—these attractive bangles that seem without electromagnetic coding can fall tickety-tick as if by accident into the widemouthed soft basket on Vola's arm.

Part Two

Vola pauses at the threshold before a rack of picture postcards. President and Mrs. Truman seated on the Key West Little White House lawn, a pelican on a treasure chest eyeing a conch shell, a blimp above Duval, the original Sloppy Joe's and the present one, the house where John James Audubon was once thought to have slept, rotting dinghies piloted here by Cuban refugees, bathing beauties and body builders, a slice of key lime pie with its recipe. Perusing the cards Vola swings her basket past the doorjamb sensors and so determines that she may exit with her booty, with impunity.

The pie picture has roused Vola's appetite. Scrimping on clothes may be a bullet she has to bite, but scrimping on food is false economy. Not that lunch need be gourmet fare. Even in the glory days . . . well, enough about that. Wasn't there an open-air corner place back on Duval?

The sidewalks are packed with families and pairs of tourists and also tradespeople, panhandlers, and OIDS cases. "Boola boola," hums Vola, "boola boola," as she cuts through the crowd, down one block, two, past an emerald shop to Pirate Jack's, a roofed bar and kitchen beside a patio with iron and glass tables under a thatch-work trellis.

Miami, Key West, Gunga-Munga, Manatee, the Everglades

Vola seats herself near a fountain. "Right with you, hon," says a passing waitress, a slight very black youngster with complex braids and a mermaid on the bib of her turquoise jumpsuit. "Drink specials on the card."

"Thanks," murmurs Vola. She dons reading glasses and slips her long feet gracefully out of her flats. "Hmm." One of those fizzes should hit the spot. Potted hedge separates the dining area from the busy pavement. On a dowel above the hedge, high enough to be out of harm's way, two parrots groom and watch passersby and lunchers.

"Sorry to keep you waiting. I'm Violet and I'll be helping you this afternoon. I would have been over sooner except for that boisterous table over your left shoulder. It's not enough that this is Papa Week, but now South Florida Rotarians convene here at the same time, because they say Hemingway was one of them. The Papa people are fairly mixed, but every Rotarian I've seen is male, white, and middle-aged, and you know what they're like at conventions. That table's only had one round and I've already been pinched twice. Oh well. What'll you have?"

"The soursop fizz, please. And then I think the shrimpboat."

"Coming right up. Nice bracelets, hon. Bet you picked them up down the street."

Vola gives a sunny smile. "You'd make a good detective, Violet. Oh, and could you ask the kitchen to go heavy on the parsley with that shrimpboat?"

Violet shrugs. "That's a new one on me, but why not?"

Nursing the drink Vola glances over a current *Key West Sentinel* and learns that despite the federal drug czar's determination to pursue suppliers onto foreign soil, to police U.S. borders implacably, and to strike prudence if not fear into users' hearts at home, and despite an impressive increase in the size and number of shipments apprehended, leading indicators over the past quarter paint a picture of exponential increases in imports of crack, smack, unapproved meds for OIDS and erectile disfunctions, steroids, antidepressants and antisenescents, and memory and hair tonics. Key West continues to be a major port of entry.

"Here we go, hon. Double parsley. How was that fizz?"

"Delicious," says Vola with great sincerity.

"Bring you another?"

"I think I'll try the sopadilla sling, and without the rum. I've had my quota. Maybe the barman will give me a break for the price. Gracious, according to the paper this place is awash in illegal drugs."

Violet's braids dance as she nods. Her eyes dance too. "Do you have a particular interest in drugs, hon?"

Vola considers. "Now I'm wondering what kind of detective you are."

Violet chuckles.

Vola continues, "Unless this is market research, or shopping."

"Legal drugs take too big a bite out of my take-home for me to think about any other kind. I don't deal either, and I don't hang out with dealers, so if the detective is you, don't waste your time. If you're a legit shopper, though, I can tell you, you can get anything you want in Key West. Okay, right back."

Since mayonnaise makes the avocado halves piled with shrimp salad unsafe to take away, Vola downs it all, even the breadstick masts and lettuce surf. "How was that boat?" asks Violet as she passes with another round for the Rotarians. "And that sling?"

"Excellent," confides Vola, slipping back into her flats. "Both perfectly delicious."

"How about a nice slice of key lime pie? It's real good today."

Although tempted, Vola declines. She leaves a generous tip for little Violet with her braids and bluish luster, re-enters the Duval pedestrian flow and then turns into residential streets where, with less resistance, she walks more slowly, swinging her arms and whistling "Makin' Whoopee," to one of the thrifts, which looks dismal and inside has almost nothing besides bicycle parts and a dented Miss Muffett breadbox with a scorpion inside that makes Vola slam shut the cover. The other thrift must be more within six blocks. Onward. Lizards flee at right angles to her path.

The Salvation Army store near a major intersection on the fringe of Old Town among a Cuban bakery, a bodega, and a liquor store, proves more promising. Used clothes demand more of a shopper's attention than new ones, and Vola easily spends a quick hour and a half choosing additions to her wardrobe. "Can you deliver?" she asks a surprised clerk at the register.

"We don't usually, Miss. Tell you what, though. You're forking over serious moola so I'll deliver when I break, in forty-five minutes. Where to?"

"The Margaret Truman Laundromat. I'll take these with me." She drops a pair of red Mary Janes into her basket. "Ask them to launder everything, for Vola Byrd. I launder new clothes too, if they've been on the rack, tried on by any old thing the cat may have dragged in."

"No problema. Listen, lady, I don't remember you. New in town? Whatcha here for?"

Vola considers. "Trying to live a good life, I guess."

"Don't you mean *the* good life?"

"Hmm. No, I don't think I do. Funny how much alike they sound, though. Okay, so thanks, pal."

"You come back to see us."

Under a flowering jacaranda Vola sits on a bus stop bench and opens a map. Murtry's looks to be ten blocks away. Vola's pink liquid crystal Timex says four twelve. If Vince actually has shacked up back there with some doxy, five might be too soon to arrive at the Court since cooling the heels with Denise and Tink, or waiting alone for them to roll in, doesn't seem exactly the bee's knees. The bus now rounding the gas station and heading this way must cross Duval somewhere nearer Murtry's. Catch it, save the feet, and while away an hour with more shopping? It stops, the door opens, but now Vola thinks no, enough crowds, and she can simply change into the Mary Janes, they won't look strange with her rose gabardine. She waves on the driver.

Halfway through changing shoes, Vola takes cognizance of her neighbor on the bench. Thirtyish, Latino, violently emaciated and splotched with blue lesions, he has begun the shuddering OIDS mambo, alternately frowning and smiling. "Gleep," he says.

"Oh," says Vola. "Oh, that bus driver must have thought I was signaling for you too. Will you be late? Can I call you a taxi?"

"Oh no no," the man says, as his dance subsides. "He knows I didn't want the bus. I sit here some afternoons is all."

Now Vola notices the man's alms cup. She roots in her basket. "I'm Vola." Under a sun visor she finds her monogrammed executive wallet. She extracts and rolls a hundred, and drops it into the man's cup.

"Hey, thanks. I'm Gustavo. Eep, sorry about the jitters, and sometimes we say things we don't mean to. It's not contagious by air though, and it's even less infectious than AIDS was, you know. Meep."

Vola shakes her head. "Poor thing. How near a cure are we?"

"Nowhere in sight. Decades if ever. AIDS was a shoo-in by comparison. Barring miracle, I've just celebrated my last Navidad on this earth."

Vola brushes lint off her lap. "How long have you yourself had this pestilence, Gustavo?"

"Vola, me personally ten months, but I tested positive eep eep a year before. I've had time to think it over. Meep."

"You've lost friends?"

"Friends, lovers. Acquaintances. My partner for the past five years checked out in November. One of us probably caught it from the other."

"I saw a woman begging on Duval this morning."

"Delta, probably. I know her. Sometimes I work over there but it's better here for the begging part. Maybe for the other too."

"Other?"

"See, the begging's gleep kind of a front. It lets me deal crack with less hassle. I'd have offered you some but I can tell it's not your cup of tea, if anything is." Gustavo chuckles.

"My stars! What are you saying?"

Gustavo manages a weak grin. "Whether it's true or not, assume it is. You know, the words of the dying?"

Vola shakes her head. "I must say, you certainly seem to be on an even keel. I doubt I'd be so chipper."

"Hey, I'm going home to my savior, Vola. Carlos and I'll have eternity to boogie in that heavenly choir. See friends, family, my pet cricket Zorro. Most everybody close to me is already there. I'll be glad to arrive."

Vola stands. "Okay, Gustavo."

"I figure it'll be like a spherical galaxy, everything tinkling, with our blessed savior and his papa and their holy amigo at the center like tungsten. Saints, Babalaws, Mother Theresa, Haile Selasse, all with their wings pasted against the globe like moths, like children with their noses against the glass, singing goodtime."

Another bus wheezes around the Exxon station. Vola decides to board it when it reaches her stop.

"Toward the edge there'll beep be accommodations for the rest of us. Spheres and tubes so that corpuscles can cruise around on underbody neon. It'll be like the best rush anybody ever had from anything, and not stopping. That has to be the best part, Vola, it won't ever come to an end. Look for me when you get up there. Maybe you'll arrive in time for our savior's twenty twenty. That'll be some party. Take care in the meantime, especially down here in Cayo Hueso."

Gustavo's arm has begun to float in the air. Vola grasps the hand flapping at its end. "I'll remember." The bus slows to a stop and its rattling doors fold open. Female feet in peasant sandals appear, thick ankles and heavy shanks, a massive body in brown crepe de Chine under black monk's cloth beneath a beaded purse and strong blunt hands, a coral brooch closing a lace collar, and now a wide neck and head, cropped grizzled hair, hooded eyes that seem to take in Vola with interest as the woman eases her bulk onto the pavement and steps aside for Vola to mount. "Yo, Carmen. ¿Como estas?" Gustavo says. The rattling doors unfold and close and the bus begins to move.

"She looked like a bus herself," Vola thinks, taking the first available window seat. "She looked interesting, too. And interested. Could she be a detective from that clothing shop? No," thinks Vola, "she didn't notice my bangles after all."

Part Two

Locals and tourists chat, expostulate, and bill and coo in Spanish, filling half the bus, which sighs and sways through green light between terra cotta walls under a canopy of leaves and flowers, and into the open alongside a cemetery of raised tombs, a fleet of shrunken marble and granite buses parked at day's end, some adorned with faded plastic bouquets. Beyond across a street stand a three-bay "eyebrow house," upper window sills visible beneath the overhanging roof, a Queen Anne house with a turret, and a Greek Revival with a widow's walk. The Norfolk pine behind them could be a giant toy Christmas tree. Three green parrots shriek and tumble in the air above the tombs.

Through another neighborhood and onto Roosevelt beside a marina where cutters and sloops ride at anchor in the low sun. When the bus stops and folds back its doors Vola hears boat rigging lines choiring in the wind. There on a near yacht Denise and Tink huddle with a portly mustachioed Latino. Vola nearly waves and calls, but she thinks better of it as the doors close. The bus trundles into a quarter of houses mostly younger than Vola, stucco flat-roofed ranch-styles in tropical colors, with tidy lawns, terra-cotta jugs, a plaster Virgin in a vitrine. Vola sees a school with a stiff oversize tiger in crumbling concrete, tall cereus and succulents, a drycleaner's with a faded wall painting of a black cat grooming her kitten, and a baseball diamond.

The bus re-enters Old Town and when it seems as near Murtry's as possible Vola descends and strides in what should be the right direction. A young mestiza mother temporarily blocks the sidewalk, maneuvering her toddler out of a videophone booth. She seems to apologize in Portuguese as the bow-legged child flaps its arms and beams upward.

Vola steps into the booth and folds shut its door. She sets her basket on the shelf and rummages for her address book and phone card. "Do we really want to do this?" she asks.

"What've we got to lose?" she answers. She keys in ooo eee ooo eee eee ooo ooo, and hears at the other end like next door tweet tweedley-deedley-dee. In the hologram niche a head materializes, Lillian Margiotta, reptilian with her delicate skin and bright black eyes. "You must be Vola Byrd. Is Vince okay?"

"He seems fine. I wanted . . ."

Lillian interrupts, "Just a minute," and leaves the niche. Vola looks at a flowered antimacassar on mulberry velour.

Off camera Lillian says, "It's the latest notch on Vince's belt, maybe looking for commiseration," and then, "Hey! Keep your paws to yourself." The light streaming in Lillian's Manatee windows looks exactly like the sunlight streaming into the booth here.

Lillian returns. "Tuna casserole. I wanted to get it into the oven because I didn't know how long we'd be," she glances aside, "consulting. How are the youngsters?"

Vola crosses one foot behind the other. "Fine too. They've been trying to make contacts. I spied them with one twenty minutes ago." Lillian fails to react, and Vola continues, "I wanted to tell you I have no long-term designs on Vince. Maybe none period. Also I wanted to see you."

A weary smile crosses Lillian's face. "And?"

"Now I'm not sure it was a dynamite idea." Vola frowns. "I don't know how I expected you to look, but now you trouble me. I wasn't prepared for beauty."

Lillian shakes her head. "Your receiver must have an enhancer. Anyway what earthly difference could it make now?"

"Mmm," says Vola.

"Did you meet Vince's neighbors the Runkles? They

say, 'In golden years, only truck with what matters,' and they're right. Speaking of look though, you seem well preserved. Divorced? Widowed?"

Vola shakes her head. "Never had the pleasure of matrimony."

"Sugar daddy then, a Hamptons estate."

Vola smiles. "Not exactly."

"Whatever. You never scrubbed floors. Well, wear your sunscreen, and make Vince and the kids wear theirs. The ozone hole's big as Antarctica today."

"Gracious me," says Vola. "Why should that matter to us though?

Lillian is looking to the side again, and she mutters, "Go ahead and wet your whiskers. This is nearly over."

Vola clears her throat. "If I had children, grandkids, that hole might weigh on me too."

Lillian shakes her head quickly. "It doesn't on me."

Just as quickly, Vola asks, "What does?"

Lillian shrugs. "Who are you, to hear my life story?"

As the women search each other's faces, an electronic voice asks Vola for another phone card. She is rooting in her purse when a movement on the screen catches her eye and she looks up to see Lillian shaking her head once more through an eddying blur which, as Vola watches, resolves itself into the fingers of a hand waving, palm out in the gesture that can mean hello but that here, Vola knows, means no, no, and good-bye. Vola nods. As if Lillian were a televangelist, Vola stretches her own opened hand forward to her niche. The hands seem to touch in Manatee and in Key West and the women search each other above their fingertips before the vaults flatten and gray.

At Fort Zachary Taylor on the western shore tourists drift toward the gate where a gravel causeway leads out of the park. In the east the sky is dimming, while cloud bars over the Gulf glow peach and orange as behind them a cherry sun ticks down the sky.

Two Baltimoreans have strolled the ramparts awaiting instructions. They perch on an overhang halfway down the southwest wall where they can survey the interior. As they know, in the nineteenth century all this stone arrived by ship, like the slaves who unloaded and positioned it block on block. When Florida joined the Confederacy in secession, a handful of Union soldiers garrisoned at Key West occupied the unfinished fort and held out six weeks, until additional Union troops could arrive. Thenceforth, with Key West the center of operations for the Union naval blockade, Fort Taylor stood guard against attack that never came. Similarly, the Baltimoreans know, the fort waited through the Spanish-American War and two world wars, and landfill that moved away the shoreline. During ensuing decades, having outlived its military usefulness, the site served for dumping until the state legislature determined that it would enter the new century as park, grounds freshly sodded, stone swept.

Tink takes Denise's hand. The ledge cools their bare thighs and calves. Across the darkening sward parents with an adolescent mosey forward, pause, and gesticulate before all shrug and proceed. Yonder by a pyramid of cannonballs two who seem older walk like longtime lovers, genders lost in the distance. Frogs and crickets have begun chirping. From stone to stone down the wall a child hops with birdlike cries. A woman and a dog on a leash watch and listen.

Denise sighs. "Tink?"

Tink feels her hand tighten, and he recognizes caution in her voice. He sighs. "Yo, babe."

Part Two

"See, I . . ." Denise bites her lip.

"This isn't about the letter, is it?"

Denise shakes her head, dark curls swinging on her brow.

"What, then, Neese?"

"See," Denise inhales. "I was thinking maybe you might like to marry me. Don't answer yet.

"I never told you, but it must have been love at first sight for me clerking temp in that convenience store. True love in deepest East Baltimore, romance made in crack heaven, freeway above and the tunnel entrance a block away, air yellow as pee whatever the hour or season. From the moment I looked up from the *People* I'd spread over the bar code reader to protect my eyes, three AM and slush on the ground, I didn't expect much business, and then the door opens and in you walk. I think it was love head over heels."

Tink remembers the cemetery he had cut through three nights straight to case the joint, yellow snow softening on the graves, sodium lamps, candy wrappers and needles. Each time behind Plexiglas the miserable storefront had been empty except for the old Paki night clerk doing accounts on his pocket calculator, until the fourth night when

Miami, Key West, Gunga-Munga, Manatee, the Everglades

Tink had whipped around the corner and in, hand already sliding out of his pea jacket, ready for bleary eyes begging for mistreatment in a face sliding off its skull. But what strange luck. At the counter in the empty store sat Neesy with jet curlicues sizing him up. Should he admit how well he too recalled the moment? The jamb mechanism tried to close the doors and then sensed him and opened again, three or four times. The electric eye seemed to have impaled him, because in his gut he felt turn something for which the name "hook, line, and sinker" now swims up.

Denise smiles. "You looked like you were losing your balance. Then you grinned, and right away I wanted you. Even if you'd treated me like you meant to treat the old Paki, I think I'd still have wanted you."

"You know I only meant to tie him up and tape his mouth."

"Whatever. Look, there go the last tourists besides us. Is it two women?"

"I can't tell. Listen, Neesy, let's move to the bottom of the wall. The park closes at sunset. If we don't get instructions in the next few minutes, let's hightail and kiss this lead good-bye."

"In a minute," says Denise. "Let me finish proposing."

"Okay."

"I feel happy. You?"

Happy? The scam seems to have hit a snag, to leave the two of them becalmed here. Have the high rollers decided they're stoolies? If so, shouldn't he just cave, because the two of them can't have many more minutes left? Or were they meant to stay here past sunset and then get ushered into the fort's dungeon, now drug traffic control central? There meet a honcho with serious money, maybe the shadowiest of all, the Italian, a corpulent old godfather who'll take one look at Neesy and start cursing because she's a ringer for the Madonna he saw picking grapes in Sicily when he was eight. He snaps his fingers and a goon presents gym bags stuffed with thousand-dollar bills.

Happy enough, thinks Tink, for a guy with the noose of matrimony around his neck and the trap door starting to creak. "Yeah."

"I think it's the light," says Denise. She looks down at the four feet with dangling flip-flops. "Anyway though, Tinker. I have to confess that the promise of riches wasn't the main reason I thumbs-upped this jaunt. Know what was?"

Miami, Key West, Gunga-Munga, Manatee, the Everglades

"Seeing old Vince one time more?"

"Close, but no cigar. That sure, and I still hope to see Lillian, but mainly it was you I had in mind." Denise's voice lowers. "You're going to think I'm a conniver."

He raises her hand and kisses it. "Connive away."

She frowns. "I mean I was conniving when we hatched our con. I wanted you to see the best real-life example I knew of a solid marriage, because then it would be easier to pop the question. Just my luck, though."

"No sweat. Try me."

"Okay then. Will you Tink let me Neesy make an honest man of you? Will you make me the happiest woman on earth and give our children a name if we have any? The bottom line is, why not? If it doesn't work out there's always divorce, plus if you have scruples about that route we'll be so rich you'll be able to have me iced. How's about it, Tink?"

Tink pulls his lip. "Those Santeria priests, what are they called?"

"Bilbaos."

"I wonder if we could find one of them down here to marry us."

"Tink, give it a rest. I'm talking reality. Mama inherited

Lillian's veil and garter, which Lillian probably had from her ma. They must still be in mothballs in the chiffonnier, along with Mama's photo album and the bottle of Evening in Paris she thinks was never opened. What a disappointment, too. It had gone off."

"No dirty pictures?"

Denise shakes her head. "Love letters either."

"That's what you were looking for?"

"Or just a snapshot of my pa. Anyway I could wear Mama's stuff. Last month I tried on a wedding dress in St. Vincent de Paul that would fit with a little work, on it or on me. I put it on layaway."

Denise shades her eyes and peers into the shadows. After a moment Tink says, "Whew. Bet you have some other cards up your sleeve there too, Neese. But if our ship comes in we won't need to buy used clothes."

"Gee, you're ahead of me. I guess we won't need Mama's confectionery either. She said we could have the reception there, even though Saturday's one of her biggest days. Jeez, we'll be able to hire out that floating restaurant down in Baltimore harbor."

"*I*'m ahead of *you*?" muses Tink.

"You know what I mean. We can invite Snake and Bobo, everybody you used to hang with. Snake can be your best man. We can tear that floating restaurant up. We can have Gramps and Lillian up, too—it's been twenty years since Mama saw them."

"Even if they're still separated?"

"He can bring Vola, a whole harem if he wants. It's our fucking wedding and he's my Gramps. So is it a deal? You want to skip all the hoopla, just do the legal, you got it."

Tink exhales into his closed mouth, ballooning his cheeks, and then releases the air through pursed lips. "Why fix what's not broke?"

Denise begins mewing. In the fading light, is there silver on the rims of her eyelids?

Tink lays an arm around Denise's shoulders and lays his head against hers so that he can whisper into her ear. "Plus, I gotta wonder what's in it for me." She swallows and barely nods. He touches her ear with his lips and turns back toward the expanse of fragrant stone, darkness, history, and minuscule songs of turf and desire. What should Tink do?

"On the other hand I ask myself, what's to lose?" She barely breathes. "So, well, okay, let's give it a whirl. Got yourself a deal, Neese."

A cheer rises from some distance away on the island.

Denise says, "Thanks, Tinker. You won't regret this."

As they search each other's eyes, too serious now for even a kiss, the walkie-talkie strapped to Tink's wrist beeps. When it beeps again, more impatiently, Tink clicks on the receiver. A woman mutters in Spanish and then says, "Okay, muchachos, we have a change of plan. My courier hit interference he didn't have *cojones* for. Par for the course, I write it off in taxes, ha, ha. So, here's what you do. Exit the fort, left on Emma, three blocks to Petronia and hang a right. In the middle of the block on your right you'll see a pig roast at a pink gingerbread. Fade into the crowd. Over."

"Check," says Tink. "Over."

"You hate to lose a good courier. He's cruising the Gulf in a shark's belly or two by now. Over and out."

The causeway rises at a modest incline from the fort to the park boundary fence. Before leaving, the Baltimoreans glance back at the site of their betrothal. Here and there above spreading shadows washes of violet tremble against stone. The sun seems to have set behind the fort, under a star already brighter than the sky around it. The night watch rattles keys. "Have to ask you lovebirds to step on through." She adjusts her helmet and dusts her epaulets. "Can't blame you for dawdling, though. The fort's at her best from here, this time of day, clear weather."

"Thanks," Denise says as they pass through, and Tink brushes off a salute.

As they advance into a street that seems to have lost all trace of other tourists, their ears flatten to catch the clink of the lock behind and the footfalls of the guard. Black residents of this part of the island stir on shanty porches lining the right of the potholed street, and perhaps also among abandoned industrial buildings to the left. Mutts worry a bone under a streetlight. Denise says, "We did come in this way, didn't we?"

"It looks different because of the light."

The curs bare teeth and shrink into shadows. The Baltimoreans proceed another block in the deepening twilight. More and more residents step out now chuckling and nodding for a breath of air. Against a stoop one nurses baby talk out of a mouth organ, and another fools with catgut. Yellow light gleams from a bleared window.

"New ground for us," says Tink when they turn onto Emma. "Know what I mean?"

He means that the two of them haven't set foot on this street before. They started playing the game on their second date, when they went into northwest Baltimore to see the zoo. When the bus crossed North Avenue he had said it was new territory for him and she had said for her too. They might have known there wouldn't be much left of the zoo, but that was okay, a lady had sold them good caramel popcorn. Since then, like when Bobo took them to a shooting gallery in south Baltimore, one or the other has enjoyed mentioning the new ground. Of course they could count this whole Florida trip, but neither has thought to mention it since crossing the Virginia line south from D.C., until now. Tink also meant that by now some of Key West feels familiar.

Who was that dude sang the country roads song, and wanted to buy part of the moon? Carl Sandburg? Denise's mother used to sing Denise to sleep with his hokey song about taking me home, and even though it was in their own apartment with blue neon shining through the lace, still when Mama had sung "take me home" with that twang like Louella Parsons with the boobs and the nice smile, when Mama sang "home" it had sounded like Mama was singing about some place other than their apartment, and like Mama knew that place, or at least had heard about it on good authority.

For a while in fifth grade this other "home" had seemed maybe where you went to kick the bucket. Anna Tagliabue's gram had left on a stretcher for the old country, and when some snot-nose asked what was happening, Anna's ma had searched for words and finally said, "Signora Tagliabue is going home." To Pozzuoli, no, on the slope of Vesuvio? A year later Denise had glimpsed another meaning for the elusive "home." Lateesha Webb, the blackest girl in the class, had taken Denise to an alley in west Baltimore to visit an auntie "so old she 'member Carolina." A disaster on the screen had prompted the faded mummy's only words. She had slid the pipe out of her mouth and pointed at the corpses with it. "Better off, now they home."

But that didn't seem exactly what Mama had sung about

either. What then? No good asking, Denise had known almost always, for even if Mama had known the answer, she wouldn't have known how to say it. So Denise had made it her own detective game she'd never told anyone about, and not even much of a game, just circling back to wonder what it could be like for a place to be new and familiar at the same time. Anyhow, this time when Tink mentioned new ground back at the corner, maybe he told more truth than ever before, and more than he meant. Engaged to be married, here's virgin territory for sure.

Denise slips her arm around her fiancé's elbow. Could "home" be marriage, with a spouse who hasn't disappeared? The sky silvers as it darkens. If only night would go ahead and fall! Tink's right, this betwixt-and-between light makes everything weird, the thoughts you have when you're neither married nor exactly single any more. At the corner of Petronia under the streetlight a golden-skinned woman younger than Denise pinches a cornrow. Crossing that alley on a moped, under another light, looking back over his shoulder, wisps of hair streaming, elbows canted, and now gone again, you'd swear it was Gramps in flight.

Miami, Key West, Gunga-Munga, Manatee, the Everglades

Ahead there, that must be firelight spilling onto the street. Smell the pig roasting.

A man steps out of the shadows. "You folks lost?" Dark-skinned, horn-rims, dark suit and tie, white shirt, burping a baby or an iguana on his shoulder.

"We're from Baltimore," says Tink. "Down for the weather, and to show somebody a letter. Do we look lost?"

The man shrugs. "It's a free country."

Tink and Denise approach the fire. A glistening pig and a kid turn on spits. Around a boom box couples and individuals dance vintage dances with Cuban and African moves. An older group in garden chairs and on a pew sways shoulder to shoulder and harmonizes. Tink pulls the chain letter from his pocket and unrolls and pretends to study it. "And the flickering shadows," sing blacks beyond the fire, "mmm, softly come and go, woe-woe." On a creaking glider two frail women in ruffles coax out an echo with ocarinas, "wa-wa-woe."

In the blackening sky among fixed stars things twinkle in flight and orbit. Addle addle splat squat, a zoot-suiter in shades sidles forward synthesizing tenor sax up and down his chest on a keyboard hung from his neck. He doffs and flips his porkpie to show a nest of paper money. Squorky orky, orky. "Say, bro, that a letter for a lady?"

Denise nudges Tink. Across flames and laughter, across electronic pop and sizzle she hears, "Though the heart be weary," old voices in old harmonies, "sad the day and long."

"Uh," says Tink.

Denise says, "Gimme five, bro. We're here to deal. And don't mind my friend. The cat gets his tongue but he's solid."

Tink nods.

"Nemmind, baby." The man shakes his hat of money and returns it to his head. "What say we three step us between these bungalows out of the light." He pats Denise's shoulder. "Me thinking he was the brains don't mean we retrograde. He just had the piece of paper. But hey, our head honcho's a broad. No flies on us." Ooky doodle-woodle. Turning to Tink, the man lays a finger against an eyebrow, nods, and nudges down the frames of his shades to look over them. "Follow us, junior," he says. "You behave, nobody gets hurt." Ooo, wonk.

"Some necktie," observes Tink.

Miami, Key West, Gunga-Munga, Manatee, the Everglades

"Junior?" asks Denise.

"Whatever." The man taps black disks into place in front of his eyes. "Korean," he explains to Tink. "Three ounces of knitted Malaysian circuitry, controls displaced onto your wristwatch. Does a sweet solo Stradivarius. On-off's on the tie pin, see? You a musician, kid?"

Denise shakes her ringlets. "He's not a kid either. Listen, whatever your name is."

"James."

"Okay, James. I'm Neesy and this is Tink."

James touches his porkpie. "Enchanté."

"Yeah, well," growls Denise. "I don't know what it is you mean by 'brains' and 'Junior.'"

"The usual," says James. "Look, there's light by the clothesline."

"One thing, though, James," says Denise. "Your people want to buy in to our letter, fine."

"More than fine," adds Tink. "Better investment than numbers, crack, and the ladies combined."

"Right," continues Denise. "Except this deal will run smoother for all concerned if you show a little respect to Tink and me both, and get outta here with hierarchy, because we put that shit behind us even before we got engaged. The brains is us both and where we're concerned there's no junior or senior. Right, Tink?"

A slow smile breaks across Tink's face. "Right on, babe."

James says, "I'll bear it in mind. Now look here." He spreads a handkerchief on the sandy dirt near the clothesline pole. "Hunker on down, folks." A rat terrier joins the humans. James flips bills from his porkpie onto the hanky, coaxes them into a stack, slaps it against his palm, and taps it with a knuckle. "Fifty grand for a copy. We don't have time for peanuts. Wanna count?"

Tink and Denise shake their heads. He lays a business envelope beside the cash. The terrier sniffs it and then limps away into the dark.

Vince turns up the collar of his lemon puckered nylon golf shirt and notches down the bill of his cap. He hunches forward as if he means to roost under the awning of a used video store. With hooded glances he notes lights in dwellings coming on, three children conspiring on the next corner. Vince steals a glance over his shoulder. Through the orange neon "Buy, Sell, Trade" he sees a tired clerk reading at a counter. Safe for the nonce. But what if that simulacrum packing real live ammo has kept a bead on Vince down alleys and around corners? Vince needs wheels, and he observes that the moped parked out of range of the store window is not locked to the bicycle rack.

Vince slips a note pad and pencil out of his shirt pocket and writes, "To each according to his need." (Who said that, one of those old arbitragers?) "My need for your vehicle," Vince licks the point, considering, "overrides much, because it happens to be a life-and-death matter. Hey, though, this is hardly theft. I mean," Vince reverses the pencil and pushes over the small page with the eraser. Musing, he applies the eraser to the window beside him, to rub off what seems to have been a fly. Inside the amber store the yellow clerk at the counter actually isn't reading, no, it looks more like he's writing. Seems to have been a party in there, long curlicues hang from the ceiling. Maybe the guy's writing thank-you notes. The thing on the glass won't rub off, it's on the other side.

Vince writes, "At an unspecified time in the near future, I'll return this convenience to this place" (but suppose there's a stakeout?) "or the island police station" (but that could be staked out as easily) "or a third location, with another explanatory note. Meanwhile, gracias, amigo."

Thrip, Vince pulls the pages free, slips them under a weathered conch shell, and mounts the moped. He shifts to "start" and prepares to pedal. These things are like lawnmowers.

The clerk in the honeyed depths—the glass must be amber, or have they glued on a yellow filter, wrinkling now and fly-specked, or is it only the glue itself, or some other amber deposit inside, so that the clerk need not actually be at all yellow—what, is he hailing from in there? Vince peers. Those party streamers look more like flypaper ribbons Vince used to hang from the ceiling fan in the barber shop, stayed sticky months until they went brittle, Lil hung up the odd one in the first Brooklyn walkup. Yes, the clerk is signaling, "Wait." Wizened little fellow, in prison stripes and a bandanna, definitely been writing on a chalkboard he now rotates and tilts up, look at that grin. Vince reads the three-word message.

He rereads it. "You're dead meat." Vince's finger touches his breastbone. Me? The clerk nods with glee.

Miami, Key West, Gunga-Munga, Manatee, the Everglades

Vince vamooses, pedaling through honey until the engine finally starts, and now let's book, goose her to the max. Wheels, don't fail me now! These lights must be Duval, but that robo-mama could pop up anywhere, but look, a gap in the traffic, one-way traffic if there's a god in heaven. Ignore stop sign, pedestrians—fishtailing, sorry pal—what'd he hoot, "Watch it, gramps"? Left, right, bumpety bump, darker here, no traffic and, firelight, silhouettes swaying, could've sworn that white face was granddaughter Neesy swimming out of the dark and then gone, must be hallucinating, bump, left, water ahead, left, water, fishing pier, space, pavement, don't slow.

This would be South Roosevelt Vince speeds along. After a few years cabbying you can't even remember what getting lost feels like, not in a city you've spent more than an hour in, or whose map you've eyeballed. Without thinking you know where you are to within a block or two. This is the beach road that circles the island, sparse traffic, RVs on both shoulders, sand beach on the right, some beachgoers in the moonlight, and the galumphing ocean, its clean breeze freer of earth than Manatee breezes, freer of industry than New York and Jersey sea air even at the limit of Vince's recollection, and salt marsh to the left, the only undeveloped patch of the island, and ahead on the left must be Key West International Airport, once a drug traffic hub and reputed to be making a comeback.

Speaking of ahead, the beach narrows and dives under walkways crossing to spidery piers alongside which, Vince now discerns, rides a rundown little flotilla of houseboats with lighted windows, clotheslines, lobster pots. Up ahead people spill onto the sand, filling up the tail of beach and, what?, joining hands, approaching the boulevard. Planning to blockade it, take Vince in a pincers movement? Think again, chumps, this cabby's shaken the mob in Park Slope on a weekday.

Vince executes a smooth U and lays down rubber on a straight shot toward the Old Town. He throws back a glance—no pursuers. Whew, he's thinking, safe for the moment, when the moped coughs and falls silent. Where'd they hide the blamed fuel gauge?

Momentum carries Vince through a quick right off the boulevard, out of sight of that rag-tag tie-dyed pack back there—some kind of wetback hit squad? The moped coasts to a stop atop a low bridge. Hell of a note. What a sky though, big moon, twinkles scattered over the black, some here and there inching their merry way above the mangrove thicket. Quiet with frogs.

Vince sighs. Why not simply abandon the blasted machine? Who could tie him to it other than the grinning shop attendant? Vince can remove fingerprints, plus it's starting to look like high time to leave this whole burg in the dust. Vince sighs deeper. Don't you ever earn the right to take the easy way out? He waves away midges. He can hide the moped in this canebrake and tomorrow send young Tink to retrieve it. Vince eases the machine off the bridge onto the roadbed, sandy gravel now. Just over there's the mangrove clump.

"Not a prudent move, Papasito."

Whaa? Vince peers over his shoulder. Movement among the girders. More of that beach crowd? No, not this band wafting out from the shelter of the bridge. "Prudent?" asks Vince. Some of the materializing faces look familiar.

"Ever hear of quicksand? What you want to leave the road for? That's no dirt bike." Full pepper-and-salt beard, fatigues, cold half cigar migrating from one side of the mouth to the other.

"I ran out of gas and thought I'd stash this here. I'm Vince Margiotta, down from Manatee on the Gulf."

The bearded man steps forward to take Vince's hand. "Fidel. Welcome, Vince, and let us fill you up enough to get you out of this no man's land. Manuelito, amigo, bring some gasoline for this gringo."

"Wait," says Vince. "Fidel? But I thought . . ."

Fidel chuckles. "Lots did. Here I am, though, big as life." He spreads his arms. "We're The Trolls, here in the mangroves by choice, and it's not a bad life. How about our chickees, mon?"

Vince bows to the trio nearest Fidel. "Evening, ladies." Arms entwined, they stand like Graces.

Fidel chuckles again. "Winnie, Imelda, Tammy Faye, meet Vince. As I was saying, we do subsistence farming and we build our own chickees."

"Chickees?"

"Thatch and berm huts like the first people in the Keys built. Colusa and Tequesta." Fidel smiles. "You probably thought they were refuse heaps."

"Tequesta?"

Fidel nods. "Indians."

"Indian huts," says Vince, now discerning more of them. "Chickees."

"Surprisingly comfortable. Jimmy calls his there 'Margaritaville.' He'll be stirring soon. He knocked back too many Cuba Libres last night."

The frogs seem louder. "Subsistence?" says Vince. "Why so much asparagus then?"

"Arafat," says Fidel, "Set this man straight."

The one in a kerchief says, "Not asparagus. Mangrove pneumataphores. Like cypress knees."

Vince is lost. "Knees?"

"Not even edible."

Fidel says, "Saltwater marsh, mon, use your head. We grow produce in raised beds. Sugar cane too. Down on your luck? On the run? Yearning to breathe free? Whatever you're dodging, you can dodge better as a Troll. Look, our old world Nestors here can go over details. Maggie," a stout woman pawing the marl, "has handy administrative experience, and Jacques-Yves," built like Vince and pursing his lips, "wrote the book about marine ecology. You can move in immediately, amigo." Fidel spreads his arms wider.

"You tempt me," says Vince. "I haven't seen such hospitality in a coon's age. Does the heart good. Could you let me have a rain check? I still have business back there." He points a thumb over a shoulder.

"Caramba!" says Fidel. "Sounds to me like love. Okay, Manuelito, let's fill the mon up."

Oily Manuelito shuffles forward with a gasoline can, waving his pitted face.

"Thanks a million," says Vince. "Any of you find yourselves up Tampa way, give me a buzz. Vince Margiotta in Manatee. When you first came out from under the bridge, I thought you were another ambush." Vince recounts his about-face on the beach road. "A rival gang?"

"Oh, that was no ambush," says Winnie.

Tammy Faye says, "That was hospitality too."

"If they saw you," adds Imelda.

"They'd've refueled you, in more ways than one. They're Deadheads," explains Arafat.

"Deadheads?" asks Vince.

Fidel says, "Groupies for the Neo-dead, hermano."

Vince smiles. "You're still drawing a blank, partner."

"You must've heard of them," calls Jimmy from Margaritaville. "They've been cranking space jam, oldies, all sorts of easy listening since before you were born."

"Fans troop about the country after them," explains Maggie. "For decades their appearances have only been announced by jungle telegraph, so to speak."

"Ze 'Eds crawl from woodwork," continues Jacques-Yves. "Sometime ze band make ze gig, sometime no. Ze 'Eds, zay remain mellow regardless."

Vince nods vaguely. He has been watching a pear-shaped woman and a seeming fuddy-duddy. "I apologize," he tells them, "but I don't seem to place you. Entertainers?"

"On occasion," says the fuddy-duddy. "Not Trolls however."

The pear-shaped woman chuckles. "We too are visiting this island. Down from Pittsburgh for the WC, the Writers' Conference."

"Drusilla and I are gathering material at the moment," adds the fuddy-duddy. "Today's assignment."

Drusilla leans forward to confide. "We're on character. 'Go out and bag some,' were the seminar leader's last words. When Elmer and I caught wind of these Trolls, we thought they were a gold mine. But you know, Vince, they haven't quite panned out. They seem a touch pawed over."

Vince smells Drusilla's perfume. "Like one of those trees that's been photographed to death?"

"Something like that. I personally was suggesting to Elmer that we call it quits when, voila!, you appear out of nowhere, and I feel like what's-her-face with the shower of gold falling into her lap. 'Trust instinct,' the seminar leader said—remember, Elmer?—'trust instinct when it comes to character.' As soon as I saw you I knew you had character I could use. Could you spare an hour? Maybe Elmer could capture you too." Bespectacled Elmer considers.

"Ah," says Vince, "actually I'm due back in the Old Town now. Tell you what, though, Drusilla. What did you say your family name was, by the way? Jones? And you are Elmer . . . Emerson? Tell you what, Drusilla, how's about if I oblige you tomorrow afternoon? Elmer too if he wants to tag along. Fourish?"

Drusilla sways. "Capital. Shall we say the lobby of the San Carlos Theatre? We can catch the Lookalike finals, and then hop over to Sloppy Joe's for sundowners."

"You got it," says Vince. "Evening, folks," he tips an imaginary hat to the figures now edging back into the darkness, "and thanks for that gas." It can't have been more than half a gallon, adding no more than four or five pounds, but Vince feels the difference as he pushes the moped back up to the center of the bridge. Not as strong as he once was. He switches on the rocket-shaped headlight and rolls forward. Halfway down, the engine catches and the light extends in front of him.

As the beam bobs westward over the beach road it enters wide binocular lenses. A good minute should pass before the old coot—who ought to be harmless, who ought not be loose on the streets after dark, whom one ought not even need notice—will arrive here, where a thickset woman's binoculars now slip into their case with a breathy clunk.

Big Carmen, aka La Gorda, the heavy perpendicular blocking access to an alley the mopedist might attempt, says, "You're history." She peels an opera bag off Velcro at her waist, opens it, and says, "Mister, you're dog food."

No rest for the weary, Carmen clucks. Bust your butt a score of years giving whatever it takes and in Medellín or

Saigon, some dive, you glance up from your keypad at the scumbag across the table, you think of the fleabag you'll retire to for a short heavy night before another stop like this tomorrow, Detroit, Petersburg, the scum across the table explaining how he botched a transfer without meaning to and certainly without skimming—no tucks for his doxy this season, he laments—yet southern rim shipments look cleaner this month, he assures you, brightening, so that his shortfall need hardly figure, and so on, exactly like your man in Berne, and you're tempted to cashier this particular scum on the spot. Sometimes you do but usually it's desist, Carmen, delegate, and so the years roll by with barely noticeable increments of security toward the time when you can lay your lonesome head down on a satin pillowcase and rest as long as you need. Of late the years have started to coast, and even the odd takeover bid, this nonagenarian cyclist and his gang, ruffles less.

Carmen raises her left forearm in a judo block and lays the silencer barrel across it. Squeeze one off into his stringy heart. Then for good measure track him as he passes and open a tunnel between his ears.

* * *

Miami, Key West, Gunga-Munga, Manatee, the Everglades

Lillian Margiotta née Valducci blots a fuchsia moue on lilac tissue she then lets eddy through a careless somersault into a receptacle of stiffened lace. A whisper of gray across the powdery black on her eyelids, a last appraisal. As she lowers lights a car outside slows to a stop and toots. Lillian sniffs. Where is it these Runkles blew in from?

Lillian has spent most of her life fending off busybodies. She swings a shawl of red roses on black around her shoulders. One thing you can say for Vince, he doesn't mind any business but his own, and barely that. Lillian exits and locks her trailerette that bravely holds its own in face of the Runkle stretch limo.

Gwen's face rests on the seat back. "Slide in, Lillian. We're going to have loads of fun. If I were you I'd think of it as reappropriating old haunts. My, doesn't Lillian look well, Brent?"

Maneuvering the vehicle onto the street, Brent yet manages a glance in the rearview. "Never better. Wish I could say the same for myself."

Gwen's face swivels toward her spouse. "He's has some odd little symptoms," she explains.

Now the car purrs down palm-lined blacktop alongside

the golf course, and Lillian lets herself relax against buttery cream leather. "Nothing serious, I hope. Of course, at our age, what isn't?"

Brent nods. "Hopefully not. Occasional tremors, but none so far at the wheel. Night sweats."

Gwen interrupts, "We won't talk about it this evening. Look, two foursomes still out."

Lillian glances at carts trundling across darkening links like stragglers to a carnival setting up beyond the horizon.

"Drowsy, Lillian?" asks Gwen. "Think nothing of it, just drift off. Here." As a pane slips up behind the Runkles a dial flutters across dim channels and settles on nearly white noise, sighs of rain.

Lillian had no intention of dozing for the short ride but she does seem to have lost consciousness for a moment, until scaly Neptune lifts his trident over his parking lot, and the rain diminishes and the car stops. It all looks the same as when she was half a deuce, no? Well, yes and no. Newly alone like this, as she feels even with these pestering Runkles, in a place she's been to a hundred times, Lillian winces when she steps out into the ranks of cars panting and almost salivating at kitchen grease in the mild air because, while the place looks the same, demonstrably, she feels inclined to think, it also looks more so, and similarly inside under the nets in the cool bustle, as if . . . what? As if what you had been discounting, black tubing on the path, the hump our party has pulled its raft onto, now without looking any different at all (your heart skips a beat) begins to look like itself. Lillian follows the Runkles to a banquette. On every side over candles and food animated old faces bob or hang in torpidity under white, gray, colored hair, wigs, gleaming pates.

When Brent returns from the tray window Gwen begins, "Do you happen to be a circuitry whiz, Lillian? We've hit a bit of a chronometric snag. Haven't we, dear?"

"You bet, dear. But let me explain. Of course you know our latest hobby. Latest and most rewarding, I might add. We decided to try our hand at a novelty item, a reverse clockwork. A mirror re-reverses it so you have forward time again in the mirror."

Gwen says, "For fun, you understand. A conversation piece."

Brent continues, "It's in the foyer, we had to move our comedy and tragedy masks. Last week several other timepieces malfunctioned."

"They stopped during the night. There was no explanation."

"We weren't overly concerned since they all were under warranty, but we were puzzled."

Gwen says, "The next thing we noticed, hands had moved."

Brent continues, "In unison, and backwards."

"You can imagine our surprise."

"We soon discovered that all of them were keeping perfect reverse time, like the novelty clock."

"We wondered whether electronic resonances could have been involved."

"You're probably wondering why we didn't think of using mirrors with these clocks too. We did."

"Except," Gwen interrupts, patting the hand that has swum in the air before Brent's face so that its forkload of calamari eases into his mouth, "except we're reluctant to embark on a hunt for materials to frame new looking glasses, each suitable for its own clock."

Brent nods, swallowing. "Plus you don't gain much duplicating a novelty item. You actually begin to lose novelty."

Lillian agrees, and suggests that the doublewide's wiring be inspected. "You have to figure obsolescence. How old is yours? Five years? Seven? It wasn't designed to handle these newer gadgets. Do you run virtual worlds? Apparently they can throw timers a curve."

"Right," says Brent, "Except, we haven't acquired any virts."

Gwen adds, "We're sure to be last on the block. What do you recommend, Lil?"

"Sorry, I'm another slowpoke."

"On moral grounds?" inquires Gwen.

Lillian thinks. "On grounds. I suppose you could call them moral. For starters, most virtuals are still pricey for my budget. But what counts more with me is the time they take. When you get right down to it, these days my budget projections with time too are on the tight side." When neither Runkle replies Lillian continues, "I wonder, though, why the time has to be real in a virtual world. If the program can put us in virtual space, then why not virtual time too? Whoever works that one out will make a bundle."

Brent frowns. "Actually you can reverse and fast forward them. The last one I played with at the rec center, Netting Butterflies, I'm edging toward an Indigo Duskywing on a log beside a stream when something big moves in the reeds. Looked like a bear."

"Oh, my," says Lillian.

Brent nods. "I hightailed it, and in the excitement of the moment flipped fast forward. High-speed butterflies blurred every which way like comets. Thought somebody'd conked me."

Lillian smiles. "The blur makes my point. The butterflies accelerated but you didn't. If you yourself could fast forward too, the butterflies would still have fluttered. You could spend a whole afternoon chasing them."

"Or running from bears," interjects Gwen.

"Running in virtual time," continues Lillian, "all in just a second of real time. I myself might be willing to squander the odd second that way. Maybe it's not possible, but technology's developing by leaps and bounds. The other day I missed a talk show about it."

"That's right," says Gwen. "We caught it, didn't we, dear?"

Miami, Key West, Gunga-Munga, Manatee, the Everglades

Brent nods. "Yeep, er, yep dear. They were talking about viruses. A version of the one that sparked the Internet meltdown could propagate in virtual worlds. They touched on bootlegging."

"Yes," says Gwen. "And also taste."

"Taste?" says Lillian. "I thought proximate senses were beyond them."

Gwen shakes her head. "No, I meant as in poor taste. One bootleg virt, what was it, Terror in Many Lands?"

"Terror Tour, I think."

"Quite frankly, it seemed strong for our stomach. I mean," Gwen sniffs, "when it comes to terror, we only hope it'll blow over before it reaches Manatee. Although you know," she flutters her small hands, "yesterday a commentator mentioned a Tampa car bomb."

"So," says Lillian, "how are you two progressing with parental grief?"

As Gwen examines her opalescent nails, Brent says, "We seem to have profited from our last chat with you, Lillian. Something happened yesterday that would've thrown us for a leap, or a loop, as recently as a month ago, but we sailed through with flying colors."

"Congratulations."

"We're fitting the mud room with track lights and Brent needed to move a hamper. We saw something crumpled behind it we didn't recognize at first. Under the dust bunnies, maroon polyester with pigskin fittings. Brent wondered whether it might be a relic from a previous occupant."

"Except it looked familiar. Sure enough, it turned out to be something we'd brought from Memphis unbeknownst, stuck to us like a burr, maybe wedged in somewhere for packing."

Gwen explains, "Of course we followed suggestions in the Chamber of Commerce movers' guidebook, and we tried to avoid null packing."

Brent elaborates. "We used towels, socks, and so forth, instead of Styrofoam peanuts."

Gwen adds, "Even though craft books have loads of suggestions for those peanuts."

Brent nods. "The wad behind the hamper turned out to be the last thing either of us would have chosen for prudent packing. Our ex-daughter's gym bag."

Gwen laces fingers under her chin. "We reminisced on the spot, fondling the bag."

"Bought," interjects Brent, "at a discount outlet. You know how kids are at that age. Gwen had found plans for a nifty pieced and quilted tote."

"With braided handles."

"But we knew the labor would be wasted, so we found something less distinctive in the mall. We'd personalized it for her with a fabric embossing kit we'd stumbled onto at the same outlet."

Lillian nods. "She inherited your athletic proclivities, Brent?"

"She swam, but not in competition."

Gwen nods. "I myself had been a Junior Nereid but no, it was the mat for my seeming daughter."

"Mat?" asks Lillian.

"She preferred mud wrestling, but it hadn't yet garnered the Olympic commission's nod. She was a medalist. Who's to say how far she might have gone?"

Oboes noodling from speakers concealed in conchs and behind fan corals segue from lite jazz into new age amid the clinks and chuckles of a busy dinner hour. As if surfacing, Lillian gives her head a little shake. These Runkles, whatever they're talking about and whatever their agenda, let them continue and, for that matter, let hubby amuse himself in the Keys and let him too fall out of love while there's time. Let the children and their children not remember me. Unfinished business never finishes anyhow, so let it go. Mmm, trust Neptune's for stewed prunes. "About your clocks, though. Instead of repairing the glitch, why not repaint the faces, so the numerals run counterclockwise?"

In early light on the boardwalk at Turtle Kraal's, Denise twirls a ringlet, alone except for perched gulls and terns and the pen's inhabitants below, a turtle older even than Gramps and Lillian, and mud cats that make the surface boil each time Denise crumbles and broadcasts a honey graham.

Whatever the future may bring or withhold, and even if St. Ignatius's wind organ never wheezes me a wedding march, Denise muses, or if it does and I should prove barren—instinctively she brushes a quick cross of crumbs across her jumpsuit bodice—whatever comes down the pike, they can't take away these nights of love and days of joy at the end of Florida with my Tink, at least I don't see how they could. All the same though I herewith put in a wish for tots, three at least, no four, half and half, a Tink Junior and a little Denise, and then maybe a Renato and a Renée, close enough so I can cosset them all like nestlings. Denise sows a last sweet handful onto the roil of mouths, shanks, and whiskers, which subsides immediately to the silt across the pen floor, except near the turtle's beak. This matinal wish for a quartet of wee Quinn-Passaros is a true wish and might come true, and nobody should be able to take it away.

Denise strolls to a table on the empty terrace. Coffee and Danish, an agreeable panorama of trawlers and cutters rocking at anchor, and an hour with accounts. This could all easily get out of hand, she thinks. Leaving Murtry's this morning she has found a good two dozen envelopes hand-delivered since late yesterday, cashier's checks, stock transfers, dollars, yen, Euros. Are local accounts monitored more closely because of drug traffic? If so, wouldn't mushrooming balances attract IRS notice? With pseudonyms, even disguises as needed, you can open accounts in new banks for a while, but the yellow pages don't list enough to absorb more than a few more days' worth. Maybe Tink's right that we should buy into an under-the-counter mutual fund run by the drug pashas. Maybe yes, maybe no, a transparent green lizard seems to allow, palpating the white mosaic tabletop.

Yesterday's income tallied, Denise spends half an hour more enjoying the view as the terrace fills. A short walk brings her to one of the last new banks where as Lola McGuire she deposits all but a few thousand. "Plan to stop with us a bit then?" asks the teller.

Denise sighs. "We'd like to, it's so different from Baltimore. For instance, my fiancé and I have noticed that you're later risers than our noisy Baltimore neighbors. Maybe we ought to stay except, I don't know. We've come into a little nest egg, and I myself may continue my education. Baltimore has a handful of universities."

"Mmm," the teller says as he guides "Lola McGuire's" receipt through a buzzing gate, "Of course we have Flagler Floating Virtual University anchored in the Bight, as well as a community college over on Stock Island. What do you hope to take your degree in? Or maybe you haven't had time to weigh your options."

"No," agrees Denise, "but I'm drawn to Wop Pop, being of Italian ancestry myself."

"I see it in your face, although I wouldn't have guessed

from your name. You might nose around. It might be offered under a different name."

"Gee, thanks, Mr. . . ."

"Call me Ken," he offers. "Or Doll, heh heh."

"Heh heh for real. Take care now, Ken."

Outside Denise strolls as the mood strikes her, safer than in Baltimore, she thinks, and freer in her anonymity and alternate identities, and with her new bank balances, enjoying the rice and beans and babies down this alley, and plantains, cyclists on this avenue and on this corner a burly woman kicking away a thin hound, flowers everywhere that open as you watch. In the shelter of a mad buttonwood Denise eases herself onto a low wall and lets slip a good balloon of thinking, about the hazy bright future that seems to hover waiting for her and Tink with offspring dimly turning in it.

To Duval, up a block, left under the neon flamingo and down a pink stucco corridor narrow enough to scratch reckless elbows, that gives onto a courtyard with lilac jacarandas and show tunes, Vola waving from a corner table, thinking the Palm Court this is not, and as for Vince's granddaughter, she has sweet eyes but it's hard to imagine what any photographer could do with her unless what's-her-face that made a name with that coffee table lemur pop-up. Flip-flops no less. Vola waves again with fingers. No Palm Court but the flatware looks clean and ladies down on their luck can't be choosy. Vola pats the chair seat next to her. "Girl talk. Hungry? Love the toes, Sugar. What's it called, Petroleum?"

"Black Opal. What looks good? Let's start with nibbles. I'll nurse a Gatorade. What's Gramps up to this morning? You could be a spy, Vola, with that hat and those shades."

Vola shrugs. "Your grandfather spent last night out on the town. I haven't seen him since he went for a stroll after dinner."

Denise frowns. "Should we let somebody know?"

"Somebody?"

Denise smiles and brushes a curl off her moist brow. "Actually, I wasn't thinking of Lillian. More police, although maybe it hasn't been long enough, unless he's had a sudden rush of senility."

Vola munches a plantain chip. "Just the opposite, I imagine, if you know what I mean. Not that I'm in any position to insist on fidelity."

"Oh, I don't know. Yesterday Tink's like, Vince and Vola should tie the knot. I'm like, *ease up*."

Vola smiles and nods. "I'm old-fashioned, Neesy. Girls my age don't get acquainted as fast as you youngsters, no matter how good a line we're handed. I must say, though, Vince has intrigued me."

Neesy nods. "If I were unattached, and if he weren't my Gramps, if he gave me a come hither look I might well go thither. Maybe even if he still was my grandpa. Just between you and me. By the way, Vola, want my parsley?"

"You haven't developed a taste for it?" Vola lifts a sprig on the tines of her fork.

"I grew up thinking of it as decoration, like frills on a rack of lamb. Raw anyway. Lillian used to serve it wilted in olive oil like greens when we visited in Brooklyn. Maybe I'd appreciate the raw more if they served it in the middle of the plate instead of on the side, and if it was less peppery."

Vola swallows. "I follow. Once upon a time I may have felt the same. But our needs change, setting aside your grandfather, some of whose haven't changed in sixty years. Regarding parsley, the decorative sustains me more now, and the decorated less, if that makes sense. Tastes change too, tolerances. With pepperiness, if my taste hasn't changed, the world has. What once seemed strong tastes bland, and increasingly I relish bite. Then there's texture. I must say I prefer curly to Italian, with all due respect. I enjoy the roughness going down, for now."

Denise watches and then says, "Confidentially, Vola, while I'm speculating it occurs to me that if I were Gramps, with a lady like you as my guest, I don't think I'd be spending nights out no matter how old-fashioned my guest claimed to be."

Vola rolls eyes. "You'll have me eating out of your hand. But answer me this. Why the Mary Worth shtick? An old fox like me has to wonder what's in it for you. Bad blood between you and your grandmother?"

Denise muses. "More like no blood. Vince is definitely my gramps but Lillian's more like somebody you meet in a friend's family. Although I like her okay and, between you and me, not finding them together disappointed me at first."

"Hmm."

"So why am I matchmaking? How's about the obvious, hope of seeing Gramps happy and safe again."

Vola brushes away an ant. "Vince is luckier than he knows or deserves, to have such a granddaughter. But, happy and safe? Forget safety, for anybody any more. As for happiness, of course you're in line for bushels, but Vince may be a different kettle of fish. For starters, I don't think he's over Lillian."

"What?" says Denise, and then slowly, weighing the idea, "Not over Lillian?"

Vola shakes her head. "No need to hide feelings on my account, dear. Couldn't matter less to me. I'm enjoying all this, especially making your acquaintance, but Vince knows I've never considered it more than a fling. Shall we ask for the tab?"

Denise glances at her wrist, where Minnie seems to direct traffic with her white gloves. "Maybe Gramps'll show up at the Opera. You're coming to the Lookalike contest, aren't you?"

Back along Margaret past the wall inset with colored bottles, and the cemetery. Wreaths and swags at one crypt surprise Vola. "I wouldn't have thought they'd have any room left. Nice place to bed down, so long as you're hurricane-proof." Right and onward between lacy wooden residences to Duval, busy and lazy in the clear sun, and across to the pink stucco building Caruso once regaled and where now spectators jostle Hemingway Lookalikes on the steps and up the gilded stair to the red plush mezzanine. Tink waves from the front row. He has saved three seats but, as the auditorium fills with no sign of Vince, it seems only right to relinquish the last seat, to what seems an OIDS-stricken young pencil salesman, whose can of sharpened Dixon Ticonderogas nearly talks as the excitement of the contest finale mounts.

A drum roll from the pit breasts house noise and both subside as the curtains part on a shallow bare stage, backdrop painted to suggest bullring stands filled with spectators whose cheers, audible over castanets and guitars, seem to greet the audience, which now applauds a dowager in mantilla and flamenco ruffles. She snaps closed her fan and curtsies. "Death in the Afternoon, thanks to the Guild. And a thousand welcomes to the high point of Cayo Hueso Invierno, the culmination of this year's Tournament of Lookalikes. Before you meet the finalists, let me introduce our distinguished judges."

House lights have dimmed. Above the floods she waves

the spot to a box at stage right. "From our Chamber of Commerce, Alice Gonzales of Island Bicycle." Flushed, fending off polite applause like a mime exploring a pane of imaginary glass. "Representing International Image Appropriation, Hiroko Tanaka of Floating World Academics." Nodding very correctly once, and again toward a whistle rising to her from the floor. "Finally, from the Papa Trust, second vice president H. Blake Garrett, today judging for his third year." A sheep dog blinking at the huzzahs and catcalls.

"Catcalls?" asks Tink, as the spot wobbles back to the stage.

"What it sounded like to me," observes Vola across Denise, who shrugs and then points with her chin to the stage, onto which amble six contestants in hunting and fishing attire, stout, grizzled, resembling each other and images for sale at the Hemingway house and on every postcard rack in town.

"Our finalists," says the mistress of ceremonies. "You'll notice greater age uniformity this year."

A corpulent gentleman behind Denise snorts, "Last year a fucking three-year-old reached the finals."

The mistress continues, "Instituted in the interest of fairness. Procedural questions may be addressed to myself at Hurricane Bob's. And now to present the awards, our reigning Lookalike, and our oldest yet, as it happens, all the way from St. Paul, Mr. R. M. Litewka." R. M. enters from stage left barking, "Hold your applause," chaps flapping and spurs jingling (a Western Papa?). "I'll tell you, one of these whippersnappers has quite a year in store for him or her." (Her?) "The envelope please. The runners-up are, third, Bob Stroud, second, Dave Riddle, and first, Horst Heimlich. You fought the good fight, pardners." Applause for the trio as it exits waving. "Better luck next time."

Vola peers. "Why the boos? Was one of those a favorite?"

Bronx cheers, boos, and rhythmic clapping and stamping erupt across the floor, and in the rear of the balcony laughter and more catcalls. Onstage the three remaining contestants eye each other and the house, as the mistress of ceremonies makes signs of supplication and shushing, and R. M. twiddles something at his collar (volume?) and plows ahead. "Now the moment we've been waiting for." But he breaks off when the spot wobbles to the nearest box, into which a small group is crowding, whose faces hush the audience momentarily. "Look!"

"That looks like what's-her-name."

"Gorby, right?"

"Madonna and Dan Quayle."

"Robocop, Imelda, Wawa, Peewee."

In the center, the famous beard and cigar. "That's supposed to be what's-his-face, in Cuba," Tink remarks, shouting because the audience has grown restive again. "Wrong contest, hang it up," some cry, and "Not even close," while others hurl insults in other languages, and some merely hoot.

The occupants of the box seem momentarily befuddled. Nancy frowns, Dutch smiles fuzzily, and the spot has begun to waver when Fidel shouts something that makes many laugh.

"Huh?" says Vola.

Tink scratches his head. "He said they're who they really are, and they're The Trolls. At least that's what I think he said."

"Gimme a break," says Denise. "Half those guys already bit the dust."

Below, some of the audience mill about the pit. On stage R. M. Litewka harrumphs and introduces the finalists, Louie Loo-eye, Brazilian but black enough to be African, J. J. Gatlinburger from Utrecht, burlier but clean-shaven (or not shaven: is J. J. the female?), and Shoji Yamamoto of Osaka, stolid and waving. "How's about a round of applause for three sterling examples of grace under pressure?" asks R. M. "Let's hear it for these three before we sift 'em on out."

The audience applauds and here and there claques gear up. The Japanese Hemingway's partisans sing a thin brisk anthem into wrist radios that seem by electronic wizardry to be transmitting directly into the hall's sound system, while down the center aisle the female Hemingway's rooters push a float with her initials picked out in purple and white hibiscus, and the black Hemingway's supporters rap dance in place following moves their favorite initiates on stage.

Meanwhile still another group elbows through a side entrance onto the floor, with bullhorns and placards identifying them as Liberal Arts Irregulars protesting betrayals of postmodernism. This group looks murderous and, whether or not they're who they purport to be, one of them, look! Tink, Denise, and Vola put heads together and point.

Miami, Key West, Gunga-Munga, Manatee, the Everglades

One of the intruders has raised to his shoulder what looks like a laser rifle and is aiming it over the chaotic floor. Toward the judges' box? No, toward the next one. Denise hands Vola her opera glasses.

In the reduced visibility of the opera the box in question seems to float like an alcove in a bank of clouds above a darkling plain where confused armies clash. A pane of bluish light angles across its front, and behind, among obscure gilded chairs strewn like undersea wreckage, in the recesses of the box a massive figure half-visible in the gloom seems to be hailing the three remaining Hemingways on stage as it, or she, moves to the rim and more into the watery veils of light. A corpse surfacing, thinks Denise, who has followed Vola's line of sight.

Tink laughs and says, "She musta got tied up in traffic, climbed the wrong stair in a tizzy looking for her pals."

"Pals?" asks Denise.

"Fidel and his crew over there. She's Gertrude Steinway, the Hemingway playmate. The house has a simulacrum, remember?"

"But I thought the real one was supposed to have gone belly up. Right, Vola?"

Vola fails to register the query. She has stood to peer better into the box whose imperiled inhabitant, she now sees, is less hailing than aiming at the Hemingways, with a purse-sized revolver, all unaware that she herself has been targeted by one of the Irregulars below. Now however the blockish dame, who seems Vola's own age give or take a decade, swarthy and well turned out in pigeon-gray crepe with over-dyed lace at collar and cuffs, seems to have been distracted, and by Vola herself, for she is looking hither toward the balcony, and so putting herself still more in danger from the laser rifle below. The wise gray eyes gaze directly into the barrels of Vola's opera glasses, and into Vola's very heart, she thinks. Something must be done.

Carmen alone in her box, with reason to believe that one of the Hemingways heads up a cartel that has rigged the contest to muscle in on her territory, has thought that, unless the rival should give him- or herself away, the most elegant solution would be to pick off all three from her box. But who is this new player at the edge of the balcony, mandrill-like with her nasal prominence? She has dropped her opera glasses, and flaps her arms as she croaks something over the uproar, "Tug," maybe? Or, yes, now Carmen hears "Duck!"

and complies, in time for a red whiz to drill the flocked panel behind the now blushing air she no longer displaces. Electricity and water sputter. Carmen squeezes off a blind shot over the rim of the balcony before she crawls past the sparking trickle onto a landing.

Pandemonium. In the lobby angry faces, raised arms, noisemakers and tin whistles, a bass drum thumping, cries. "Bum rap! Can the judges! Recount! Up yours!" Popcorn and confetti shower Tink, Denise, and Vola as, hands locked, they thread through the milling crowd. Immediately in front a pear-shaped lady on the arm of a portly gentleman says over her shoulder, "Quite a mêlée! When we encountered those Trolls yesterday we found them decidedly more rustic, didn't we, Elmer?" He doffs a boater over his shoulder to say, "We dropped in today unprepared for such disorder, to see a mutual acquaintance, Mr., oops, ta-ta, folks," as the crowd shoulders him and his companion away, and Vola, Tink, and Denise to an exit.

In the bright afternoon on Duval under an airy blue sky flâneurs jostle panhandlers, shoppers bustle, and cyclists loop through the file of cars and pedicabs. Good nature prevails despite the angry crowd spilling down the steps of the opera. With guayabana sno-cones, Denise, Tink, and Vola confer under a royal palm. There seems no way to make sense of the disruptions, no consensus even about what has happened, except that Vola's warning seems to have saved one Troll's life.

Vola laughs. "You wouldn't expect such a heavy-set lady to move so fast, not at that age. So how about a reward for La Byrd? Neesy, let me treat you to some footwear. Vince's treat too, since we'll use his wad. The flip-flops are fun, but you might need something more substantial in a pinch. Say a nice pair of wedgies. Tink, can we girls trust you to your own devices for another hour or two?"

"Actually," says Denise, "I was thinking of checking out the university. Is there still time? Tink, you could chaperone us girls there, and then we'll ditch you and swing past some shoe shops. Then what say we all meet at Mallory Square for the sunset? Gramps might show up there too. Didn't he mention it?"

"University, Babe?" asks Tink.

"FFVU. Flagler Floating Virtual. Who knows, I may enroll and further my education now. They must have correspondence courses, or I could find equivalents in Baltimore."

Vola and Tink exchange glances, shrug, link arms, and follow Denise to the water's edge and, ignoring posters announcing that no visitors may be admitted during winter break, over a gangplank onto the Flagler raft. Inside, transceptors hang like oversize curtain rings from a rod. The trio slides off three, dons them like halos, and strolls down a musty cool arcade, up a short stair, and into the lobby of an old hotel or cinema, lights low, marble floor deserted, columns branching into stonework arabesques on the domed ceiling.

"What's this?" asks Vola. "Seed?"

Beside a chocolate cork bulletin board a metal rack displays paper packets illustrated with pictures whose colors look both fresh and old. Early colors, Denise terms them. Vola steps forward. "Wonder if there's any parsley. Are they this year's? Are they for sale?" She peers at a label atop the rack, and then at some of the packets. "What do you aim to study, Neesy?"

Denise says, "Maybe a class about reading the *Promessi*

Sposi. Mama gave me her printout but it's all in Italian. Or accordion maybe. Why?"

"Because these," Vola's finger has slid to the bottom row of packets and across, "appear to be courses. They're current but no, they don't seem to have what you need."

Tink says, "More something she wants. Right, Neese?"

"Need, want," Denise shrugs. "What's in here?" The ornate doors labeled "Auditorium" seem locked, and little if any light comes through the eye-level panes. Denise leans close enough to shield her view with a frame of hands, thumbs down her cheeks, short nose grazing the pane.

"Closed for break, folks." The voice issues from across the rotunda, between green and tan columns. Denise turns, as do Vola and Tink, to see shuffle from shadows an ancient custodian with bright eyes. "Under lock and key. In fact, you're not supposed even to venture this far in."

"Nobody here but you?"

"You can hear the mice dance. School resumes Monday. Come back then for a tour, labs, book rooms, dormitories. This was the lobby when Mr. Flagler built the place as a hotel in the northern part of the state, non-virtual then, justly famous for the Moorish arches and mosaics."

"Excuse me but, are you yourself virtual?"

"No sirree, young man. I'm actual as the day I was born. I suppose you'd say the same for yourselves."

"Er . . ." says Tink.

Denise stands fetchingly, feet turned out, fingers interlaced as if nestled in a tutu. Trespassing is illegal and furthermore this institution might network with others in Baltimore. "You must have been with FFV a while. I bet you enjoy your work. Lucky they don't have mandatory retirement."

"Don't know about luck. Pension plan's nothing to write home about, but I reckon I could live on it. Maybe I should step aside like you suggest, and give the work to somebody younger."

"Oh, I didn't mean that."

Denise's confusion prompts Vola to join the conversation. "You never get an itch to travel?"

The custodian's eyes twinkle. "There's itches and itches, missy. Stop by this evening, I'll tell you more."

Vola raises eyebrows and is about to reply, as Denise and Tink feign deafness, when a distinct "Ping" wobbles through the domed space. The custodian smiles. "Enemy sonar."

Vola laughs. "I'd have said radar but you're right. I recognize the sound from war movies." She smiles. "Real movies. These kids are too young for the thrills we had going out to those palaces Saturday night. In fact," she surveys the stately interior, "this reminds me of them."

"Excuse me," says Tink. "Did you say sonar?"

The custodian nods. "You didn't realize we was submersible? I wouldn't have taken her down had I known you was aboard."

"Down?"

The custodian inspects a gauge set into a column. "Four and a quarter fathom. I give her a test run every day or so. During session we stay down weeks. Runs on nuclear."

Denise says, "We're underwater now?"

"Just off the dock, here in a trench I like to ease her into. Sitting on the bottom, in fact."

"Excuse me," says Tink. "About that sonar?"

The custodian shakes his head. "Probably a rival institution of higher education. They won't pick us up so long as we lay low."

Tink bridles. "Listen, mister, we want out of here. I hope you won't be insulted if I do without this fucking halo," he says, reaching for his transceptor.

"I wouldn't do that, son," says the custodian, in such a way that Tink's hand falls without having crested his ear. The custodian continues, "The other sub's already out of range. Give me five minutes and I'll have you back on dry land."

On the dock the trio waves to the custodian as he disappears beneath the FFVU portal. "What now," asks Vola, "shoes?"

"Great. Tinkie-pie, can you stay out of trouble for an hour?"

"Hey, Vola's the dark horse. You plan to drop back for a beer with that dude?"

"I suspect not. I wasn't sure what he had in mind. Plus, it would feel like cheating. Never mind that I'm being stood up myself."

Denise clucks. "It's Gramps's style. We can ring the

trailer court from Duval, maybe he'll have left word. Wedgies, you think? Tinker-bell, sweetie, see you at sunset."

Shopping, Denise and Vola have more to discuss than they would have thought possible a few hours ago. In The Well-Heeled Octopus, surrounded by a flotilla of shoeboxes bearing points of tissue like flames (deceased Japanese infants, Denise thinks, set adrift on wave-patterned carpet, and Vola thinks, herring boxes without topses), while a sales boy kneels before them with a pearly shoehorn they disagree amicably about Neesy's engagement.

In Vola's opinion, now that the chain letter has assured Neesy a substantial nest egg, it would be wiser to remain a free agent. "You're young," Vola explains, and she observes that, while Tink seems a good chum, there are more fish in the sea.

Neesy brushes these objections aside. "There'll always be more fish. No, I know Tink doesn't always have his best foot forward. There's no way you can see him like I do."

"Which is how?"

Neesy focuses on the part down the center of the sales boy's bowed head. She says, "He's my Prince Charming. Plus, I want to start a family soon. You never know."

"Know?"

"What's around the corner. So why wait?"

"Fair enough," says Vola, "but I can't see why anybody wants children."

"Lots do, though."

"I know. Can you explain it?"

Tink has made his way south into an Old Town backwater, down a narrow street of peacefully decaying shotgun cabins behind traveler's palms with wind-shredded pinnate leaves spread like fans. A gazebo draws his attention to a bungalow engulfed in rose and cerise oleander and hibiscus. "Enter," says the English line of a plaque that repeats itself in other languages, swinging from the sky-blue tongue-and-groove porch ceiling. Tink complies, and also with the implied "without knocking."

What is this room, with blue armchairs threadbare under antimacassars, iridescent vases, and irregular gray pine floors splotchy with damp and old spills, a flophouse? A waiting room, while they reset your timing or replace transmission? Except, no tube or Muzak or even a goldfish, only a murmur from the back like rainy voices.

Through the arch a dining room, although your nose tells you no meals have been served here in years. Green and purple late light through lace and foliage at windows, wooden fruit in a bowl on the table. Down a hallway lined with velvet portraits of Brando, Taylor, Elvis, the murmur resolves into rain and voices. "Carmen's offed the dude but apparently he has cohorts, Chiquita Banana voice-mailed. This thing's about to blow."

"I'm hip. Chiquita say where they're holed up or what monikers they're using? No problem, they'll eventually tip their hand."

"One's calling herself Lola McGuire. They could be connected with the Heads squatting by the airport. Supposedly they're into market research for an OIDS med."

"Steroids, I heard, or an Ecstasy spinoff. Grapevine predicts a major transfer today at Mallory. Could be the med or its formula. A tong's nosing in too."

Tink coughs before proceeding into what proves a study. It feels more lived-in than the front rooms, with a Spanish desk, high-backed and occupied rattan armchairs, and beside the window a mechanism with water dripping into a trough, producing the sound of rain. One of the room's three wizened pinochle players says, "Welcome. Feel free to look around. We're usually closed by now but Tennessee never stood on ceremony. His rain machine brought on throes of composition. Like Heine's rotten apples."

"Tennessee?" Tink asks.

"Plays. You must've seen some, *Cat*, *Streetcar*."

"Plays," muses Tink, "not gridiron. No, I can't say I ever saw one, unless music videos count. So this Tennessee wrote *Cats*. My Baltimore neighbor Ms. Garvey went to Niagara for her second honeymoon and her old man took her to see *Cats* on Broadway. Big spender, except a month later he'd hit the road and taken her life savings along for the ride. I guess *Cats* is about the six-toed Hemingway ones.

"I never got to Manhattan myself, although I should be able to swing it now. If *Cats* is still running I'll take it in for the honeymoon. I'm getting married. Did they make this *Cats* into an infomercial?

"So did this Tennessee pal around with Daddy H. at Sloppy Joe's?"

"Listen, sonny, you can get cassettes on Duval, answer all your questions."

"Check. Who are you then?"

A glance flickers among the three. "Friends of the estate. We used to visit back when."

"Okay," says Tink. "Beg your pardon. Didn't this Tennessee guy get wiped out by the first retrovirus? Maybe one of you's his ex. Listen, guys, I'm down here offering a fantastic deal I'll cut you in on, for Tennessee's sake. Ever hear of a chain letter?"

Another glance flickers among the sedentary gentlemen, each with a pencil moustache and lacquered hair.

Today the sun will set at shortly after six, and by five crowds have begun to gather in anticipation of that event off the northwest end of Duval, where Old Key West reaches farthest into the Gulf of Mexico. Here the street debouches in Mallory Square, a tangle of curio shops and eateries, its cobbles and balconies thronging at most hours. Beyond, on the Gulf margin, where the population usually thins, toward sunset it reaches peak density. Past a weedy parking lot and a couple of failed businesses lies an asphalt promenade where all day vendors have plied wares under fluttering awnings. Now others are joining those peculiarly hopeful or desperate ones in a colorful phalanx of sno-cones, cotton candy, taffy kisses and corn dogs, fresh-squeezed juices, incense, dyed sea oats and dried and fresh flowers, not to mention T-shirts. The vendors hawk espadrilles, Panamas and whimsical bonnets, seashell jewelry and fish and gator neckties, as well as brooches, patches, and other costume pick-me-ups, plus gags, photoluminescent posters, electronic statuettes, dream notebooks, spiky amber globes that must be blowfish, sunscreen, blue popsicles and black shark teeth, and other souvenirs and artworks for the gathering crowd, and some OIDS victims beg alms despite municipal regulations.

In a tradition Key West wears as lightly as any, tourists and locals gather here for sunset, all ages and races, speaking dozens of languages. Adults stroll with dogs and children on leashes, while wilder freer children chase through forests of legs. One matter-of-fact pigeon pecks apart a puff of buttered popcorn, others preen, and still others step between cartwheels, lifting dirty pink feet over obstructions.

The fluid crowd slows to standstills around performers, a juggler in motley, a magician making people laugh like tropical birds when he pulls colored silks out of their noses.

The crowd thickens to a pickpocket's paradise where a housecat jumps from pedestal to pedestal through a flaming hoop its sequined trainer holds. Elsewhere vocalists and instrumentalists perform partitas and sea chanteys, they too entertaining for handouts. Meanwhile at the breakwater families and couples choose vantages, standing at the edge or seated, legs dangling above the slosh, facing into the Gulf and the low sun, shading eyes and throwing bread to terns and gulls.

Denise in new chestnut eel-skin lace-up sandals, flipflops in a beach bag, searches the crowd and gently evades a toddler who wants to climb her leg, as Vola backs out of reach and whistles for parents to retrieve the tyke. "Tell me you don't have your sights set on one of those, Neesy. Say you were pulling my leg before it pulled yours."

"No, Vola. For real. I want at least a little girl and a little boy. Diapers don't faze me."

But where are Tink and Vince? Tink should arrive soon, unless he's here already. A predetermined landmark would have been prudent, but how could one have foreseen a population so dense and festive? "Where are those boys?" asks Vola.

As if in answer, between a cartoonish uncle urging repentance with sandwich boards and a swaying quartet of Deadheads, a glimpse of Tink munching a sub as he strolls away at an angle. "After him," urges Vola. "I'll meet the two of you in ten minutes."

"Here?"

"By the fire-eater. Hurry, girl."

Tiptoeing for a better view, Denise dodges through disgruntled Hemingway Lookalikes into a gap that seems to be drifting in Tink's direction. When the interstice veers, Denise must breast the swirl of humanity. Running is out of the question and ditto for making calls audible more than a few feet. Disheveled, sweat beading on moustache and forehead, Denise fights onward, sometimes slowed by the crowd and sometimes accelerated, and sometimes swept into a detour.

Tink too thinks it would have been wiser to designate a spot on the promenade for the reunion. Still, he thinks, chance should make their paths cross and, if not, hey, they can catch sunset separately and compare notes.

"Meep meep," says a person behind Tink. "Do you mind, pal? I said, meep meep. You're blocking traffic."

"Sorry. Here, squeeze through." This could be a fucking home game at the old Memorial Stadium, Tink thinks, when we're hot, with maybe a couple of Greek town street festivals mixed in. Except for the good weather, plus the Key West underclass seem not to have crawled out for this. So that's two good reasons for being here, Tink thinks, rather than chugging a lug with Cooter and Bobo and Tiny and Snake at Ma's Hole on North Avenue. Cooter'd call this Grope City, though.

Vola meanwhile, peering left and right, catches in peripheral vision a lamppost directly behind, green cast iron. Selectively submitting to bumps and nudges she edges back and feels the knobby column between her shoulders and buttocks. The crush reminds her of pre-9/11 Times Square New Year's Eves, and televised Japan and Calcutta. "The population explosion," she sighs. You hear all the time how crowded the future looks despite the colonies and incarcerations, the shrinkages and so forth. Hard to believe even OIDS can make a dent, even assuming some truth in rumors about the engineering of this epidemic, although here Vola is inclined to demur because, after all, why not tailor a virus that would sterilize men or, better, a virus that could take away their need to poke. Vola clucks. Won't we ever have a less gross way to maintain the species?

On the Gulf the sinking sun itself seems to blush at the freedom of Vola's speculations. She backs half a step more, going onto tiptoe and sliding up the lamppost. Over the river of heads and shoulders she sees glassy blue green water, empty except for a becalmed sail and dolphins farther out.

Directly below the sun lies empty horizon, featureless you'd say with some assurance even though a quirk prevents the line from being securely grasped by vision, Vola's at least, sharp though it remains. She must shade her eyes to look at the sun's destination a hair south of due west, she supposes. Is she sighting toward Texas then, or Mexico, or both? The lines running from Vola's pupils to where the sun will set do not in any case touch that land, whatever its name. In a sense, Mexico and Texas hang below, out of sight, less by virtue of mere distance than because sightlines on their own go straight as they can.

Could she see the land if this were Jupiter, the planet and not the Florida town? Vola shakes her head: not conserving proportion. Never mind that the surface would drop fewer feet a mile, there'd be more miles between Key West and Corpus Christi, assuming proportionality. Still, if the earth did grow beyond a realtor's wildest dreams, even sightlines would bend, as Vola understands it. Standing here with the right spyglass, and low enough air pollution, she'd see past Corpus to Baja, the Pacific, pagodas and Buddhas, and eventually the lamppost and part of the back of her own head. Except, she wonders, what then would happen to the sunset?

Up from the cobbles a shrilling seems to drill directly into Vola's molars. A pale three-year-old shrieking from sheer *joie de vivre* tears across a momentary opening in the crowd. Nothing would be easier than to ease one long foot across the nuisance's path, but before she has a chance even to restrain herself a cobble sends the child sprawling and wailing, and almost immediately into Vola's arms. "Shh, dear. Who do you belong to?"

"Please? Thank you. Please?" The distraught adults appear not to know much English. As Vola gives the mother the scarcely bruised child she notes the woman's bad teeth, the dirty creases in her white neck, the scabby clothes. The man with her extends a supplicatory hand. "Please?" Teeth as bad, cheeks as hollow. Vola decides against generosity. She herself, for heaven's sake, teeters on the brink of the underclass.

The man seems to understand. "Thank you," he says. Resigned, he turns. The mother with her child is preparing to follow when something utterly un-businesslike possesses Vola, and she tucks a crumpled hundred into the woman's breast pocket before shooing her on her way.

As Vola watches the family struggle into the crowd, waves of humanity close behind it. By now the bottom of the clear red sun seems to touch the immaculate horizon. Not darker yet but cooler, air and sky increase in transparency, and the hubbub quietens. Over the fire-eater's mouth his whooshing column stands colorless. Vola heads there through motionless sunset-gazers, some of whom mildly protest her passage. "Hey, lady, it's happening. Where's the fire?"

Where, indeed for the fire-eater holds his breath like a deferential dragon. Vola can keep his spangled turban in view by weaving her head from side to side like a Balinese dancer as she pushes onward, excusing herself and blocking with forearms. Only a step or two more.

Except that, through an opening to the edge of the breakwater, the sight of activity stops Vola in her tracks. She sees Hemingways with a tripod supporting an instrument they aim toward the water, the Japanese one turning a handle on its side. It looks like a laser cannon. Fishing here, at this hour? "Hopefully not for dolphins!" Vola thinks, and nasal echoes have scarcely died in her mind's ear when the thin Hemingway pirouettes three paces from his fellows and stands hand over heart as if for the national anthem, facing not the sunset, which might occasion understandable reverence, but more or less Vola. The man's white T-shirt of its own accord seems to turn its wearer into a tie-died Deadhead, as a red sunburst blooms from under his flattened hand.

This Hemingway sways and topples into the arms of a bystander, ignored by his fellows who fire with still greater urgency at something Vola can now make out, a small powerboat crossing the water. Vola's hand in her beach bag closes on something cold and heavy, opera glasses. She raises them to her eyes and the whole sky goes green.

Applause along the waterside, cheers, whistles for another sunset, and for the legendary green flash thought fabulous by many, including some lucky enough to have seen it, unlikely as it seems and so quickly over. Some here today, intent on not missing the sun's last wink, see the flash without registering it. Others who take in the tilting green still turn to neighbors for verification. Others blink to restore vision, and shrug off a momentary chill.

Denise, having pushed to where Tink stands in conversation, hands behind his head as if for a frisk, registers the green subliminally if at all, as an emanation of fatigue from Tink's interlocutor. She sighs. "Gramps! We almost reported you missing. What have you been up to?"

"Catting around, huh Vince," offers Tink. "Side action. I'd lay money even if we weren't flush."

"Gramps?" insists Denise, laying a hand over her fiancé's mouth.

Vince regards the young pair. "It's a long story. How much time you got?"

"For you, Grampsy? All the time in the world."

At the white double-wide in Manatee, Brent Runkle on the patio jiggles sirloins in their marinade in an earthenware dish on the tea wagon he has moved to an edge of the brickwork, beside the fireplace adorned with coquina flowerets and starfish, where a braise waits. Hidden speakers emit champagne polkas chosen for this season of carnival and wedding anniversary and Valentine's. In honor of the last, Brent has prepared chicken marinating in their own bowl where they have steeped overnight. He loads hearts and veggies onto skewers and lays them on the grill.

Gwen glides over brickwork in a peach caftan appliquéd with mauve musical notes, and Brent in chef's hat and apron printed in witticisms, over lemon and tangerine Hawaiian rayon shirt and khaki Bermudas, responds with a kick and turn mastered in Tennessee and soon to be reborn in a zydeco exhibition at the senior center.

"Smells yummy," purrs Gwen. "Sundowner?"

"Love one. I've scooted the bar a touch. I thought, the hookups are there so why not use them. Plus . . ."

Blinkered with glistening hair, Gwen stirs old-fashioneds. "Plus?"

"I needed the other power for your anniversary surprise there."

"Casper?"

"Ha ha. I didn't know what to cover it with so I thought, why not a pillowcase."

"I'm dying of curiosity. Here we are." Gwen sets Brent's beverage on the tea wagon. "Oh, have we burned our knee?" Both peer at the splotch until, biting the bullet and raising heads (bumping noggins gently), they begin, "I've been meaning to," and "You don't suppose," before, silent again, they touch similar new discolorations elsewhere on Brent until they are ready to look one another in the eye and confront the issue. "I've been reading about it on the sly, Brent."

"Me too. In fact, I've had a blood test." He tosses back a swallow of old-fashioned. "It seemed only sensible. After all, I said to myself, this could be anything, fungus a new resident left in a locker. I didn't want to burden you."

Gwen mouths "No."

Brent turns kebabs. "Your liquid foundation has helped my masquerade," he confesses with a chuckle, "but in front of this grill it melts."

"And," Gwen whispers, "the test results?"

"Day after tomorrow."

Gwen says, "We'll keep fingers crossed," brightly crossing two and waving them at Brent.

"Yes, and if the news is bad, we'll consider it our next adventure."

Gwen nods feelingly. "One day at a time, Brentie."

Brent nods. "What's on for tomorrow?" He arranges the kebabs on crackleware and lays hissing steaks onto the grill.

"Er," says Gwen, "you'll never guess what I saw from the boat ramp on my way home from the manicurist. I'd slowed because I noticed carnival decorations. The theme seems Mexican this year, skeletons and so forth. Then I noticed a crowd. I slipped over for a look of my own and, what do you suppose? An actual manatee, Brent. Basking and munching aquatic greens."

Brent muses. "Extant here still, then?"

"I too would have said extinct. Pepito from Neptune's was there. He had groceries, and he tossed out an iceberg head and a couple of alligator pears. Must've flummoxed the manatee. It dragged itself into the water and vanished."

"Big?"

Gwen considers. "Bigger than anything else I've noticed there, but I don't know how big they grow. It seemed adult."

"Hopefully not the last. But to return to my question of a moment ago, what's on tap for tomorrow?"

Gwen sighs. "Maybe it's not quite the ticket now. We have an appointment to view our resting site. I asked Lillian Margiotta to join us because I thought it might galvanize her to start putting her own affairs in order."

Brent turns the steaks. "Order?"

"Help her put that tiresome Vincent behind her. I thought the contrast with our own future eternal solidarity might clear the air for her."

"Might well." Down the lawn an egret lands to browse in puddles.

"Also, I mentioned our outing to Pepito. You remember he glimpsed her with us at Neptune's. We chatted about the difficulties of living alone. It gets old, he said. What with one thing and another he said he might drop by to look at a plot for himself tomorrow. He has deceased exes interred in two states, a cremated one in Europe, and a fourth who might be any number of places by now via posthumous organ donation. I said, just think, she could show up in Manatee and you'd never know. He has no final arrangements since they all had remarried, and he's childless." With a melancholy smile Gwen lets her head tilt back. "Given the circumstances, though, we can reschedule. But when do I get to see that prezzie? Something you've made yourself?"

Brent shakes his head. "Although I did order it from one of our catalogues. It's something we can both enjoy and, should I depart sooner than we'd hoped, it will stand you in good stead."

"I'm dying to know!"

"Yes, dear," says Brent. "And let's keep with the plan for tomorrow. Steady as she goes."

An unfamiliar ratcheting comes from beyond Lillian Margiotta's bedroom door. Wait, she thinks, struggling to stay an instant longer with dissolving shreds of a dream, about a dish of worms and someone near the ceiling, or was it sealing wax? Except that, can she have overslept? Ratchet ratchet, and now a flutter. "Cerbero," she calls, and listens to his nails as he trots from the next room to the Murphy bedlet, on which he lays his muzzle. Ratchet ratchet, whir, flutter. Lillian's heart flutters. She smooths out one of Cerbero's ears and pats his head.

Miami, Key West, Gunga-Munga, Manatee, the Everglades

The noise stops as Lillian slides from her bedclothes. She and her new wire-haired terrier pause at the threshold of the live-dine cubicle. Brimming with dappled yellow and green morning light, the silent room works a quick enchantment, as if it were an illustration in the best possible book of fairy tales and she a child. Nothing seems disturbed, and for a long moment it seems nothing could be disturbed here. This could only fade, Lillian thinks, like the illustration.

Ratchet, ratchet. Lillian follows Cerbero's gaze to where a sheet of paper appears on the wall and flutters to the floor. Kneeling, she reads "Page 3" printed and below that, in a familiar hand, "Ciao amore. Vince. Arrivederci." Lillian recalls no mention of a concealed fax receiver. Can the agent have been unaware, perhaps even the previous owner? Lillian scoops up two other leaves.

"Sleep well, Cerbero? Ready for breakfast? I think we should move our walk up half an hour today, and then you can hold the fort while the Runkles ferry me to the boneyard." The tail wags. "Oh, you'd enjoy accompanying us. You'd think you had died and gone to digger heaven. If we were taking my car I might risk it, just to see your face." The Runkles' faces would be a sight too, should one whistle a muddy hound into their sedan.

Later, in the drive, Gwen's face beneath flowered straw turns toward the trailerette and then toward Lillian in the back seat. "We didn't realize you had a guest, dear. I saw the curtains move."

"No," says Lillian, "that's only Cerbero."

Gwen exudes bright inquisitiveness.

"My watchdog," explains Lillian. "From the pound. Still young enough to feel concerned about Mama when she leaves him on his own. You two ever try a dog?"

Backing out, Brent says, "Funny you should ask." Warm though it is, he wears jaunty white silk around his dry neck.

Gwen concurs. "Isn't it funny. Why, just yesterday . . ."

"It was our anniversary," explains Brent. "We have a tradition of offering each other surprises."

Gwen elaborates. "On alternate years. Love tokens, you might say, even after all these years."

Easing onto the pavement, Brent nods. "Fun, silly, practical or not, they're always original. We have a scrapbook you must see."

Gwen continues, "You'll never guess what this one," nodding toward Brent, "selected this year. He presented it at our cookout yesterday."

"The weather was good," Lillian observes.

"He had it under a little shroud on a stand like a work of art. After the unveiling I said, 'It's lovely, but what is it?' He explained that it's a third-generation electronic watchdog, programmed to bark should an unescorted stranger approach our double-wide."

"It analyzes air samples and vibrations. Cutting edge and pricey enough not to be guarding many other Manatee hearths yet."

Lillian shrugs. "You'll save on food and flea powder. What's its name?"

"None yet in English. Just a product number."

"No, dear. She means the name we gave ours. Brent asked me to name it and I chose 'Tyge,' to commemorate Brent's shoe career. Look, the memorial garden."

They cruise past chaste stone and exuberant holograms on well-tended turf interrupted with recent interment sites blanketed in flowers and imminent ones agape, to a double plot shaded by a willow. Brent and Gwen lead over the grass to a shrine of white composition marbloid, he explains, veined with translucency. A dome rests atop eight fluted columns ringing what might be a birdbath except that its polished surface proves convex with an incised inscription, "Love Always. The Runkles." Lillian looks up between the columns at the clear sky. "Oh, dear," she thinks, as she feels a prickling in her eyes.

"We designed it ourselves," explains Gwen. "You see, we only have each other," she and Brent lower their eyes, "and we refuse to console ourselves with any . . . you know."

"Stories about afterlives," says Brent.

Gwen nods. "It seemed all the more important to know we'd be together in a secure resting place."

Lillian says, "I wonder how many in Manatee console themselves with hereafter stories. Not a majority, I'd guess, whatever we may say."

Brent says, "Maybe, maybe so."

Gwen adds, "It's not something we discuss much."

Lillian continues, "Without those stories, you might not expect the resting place to matter."

Gwen says, "Except the effect seems the reverse. No, dear?"

"Now that you mention it."

Gwen continues, "Whatever arrangement you and Vince once had now being moot, it occurred to us that if you don't have your own site, ours might inspire you. OIDS hasn't hiked plot prices yet here, so it's a good time to act. Mind you, the adjacent spaces are occupied, so we couldn't stay back-fence neighbors in perpetuity. Still, think how cozy, a lane away."

Lillian says, "I grant I should attend to it."

"If only for, for your children's sake," says Gwen, lowering her eyes again. A trick of the light glistening on the powdered lids makes them seem not quite opaque.

"Who's this?" asks Brent. "Pepito?"

In a convertible, waving as he eases to a stop and steps out, Pepito, dapper in a Panama and khakis, expresses suave admiration for the Runkle site as well as businesslike interest in the proprietors' terms. Pepito also makes courtly moves toward the newly unattached (as Gwen manages to mention) Lillian. She for her part could overlook the tobacco on Pepito's fingers and dentures, so long as there were no implied contract, and were she thirty years younger, footloose and fancy-free. As is, she continues to seem preoccupied, or dull—inattentive in any case and not in the least encouraging—and persuades the Runkles to return her to the trailerette with a joyful canine at its window. "Many thanks. You've been kinder to an old woman than she deserves."

While Lillian's new housemate rolls on grass and noses under hibiscus she, in an ancient porch chair of aluminum tubing webbed with synthetic mesh, looks over her ex's fax.

"Carissima, you wouldn't believe what I've been through down here. Mortal peril, and the danger may not be over, but I'm still kicking. Don't worry about our granddaughter either. We're all okay."

"All, humph," says Lillian.

"We plan to start back in a day or two. The youngsters have business in Miami, but I expect to be home in a week.

"I'm assuming this letter makes it through, by the way. The kids' laptop's fax accesses a universal directory. You didn't tell me your little nest could receive. Makes me wonder who else might be faxing you.

"Here's a news flash. The spring chickens I'm touring with have decided to tie the knot. I've given them my blessing, as if they need it. They're rolling in loot. I've been thinking about the vows they'll make. Wouldn't it be funny if they meant them. Then I wondered if there might be a way to help them see what it's like to really mean something that matters. I meant my vows with you. So I wonder about you."

Before perusing the second page Lillian watches Cerbero on the lawn. He catches her eye, cocks his head, and then with a wag of his tail bounds after a sparrow, happy for you to join the play and happy when you decline, instantly comprehending and accepting your decision.

"Could it be you didn't really mean your vows in Our Lady's with your sainted mother and your father, the lace falling over your thin wrists? No, you must have meant what you said, Lilliana."

Lillian sniffs. Didn't we say cleave only? Christ almighty, she thinks. Like scraps of a dream, fragments of the Brooklyn chapel swim in her mind, polished bulbous wood, the posy.

"So what's gone wrong, me? I don't think so, but I can't believe you've changed all of a sudden either. Are you testing my love? Or maybe the ordeal has no explanation. When I get back we can talk. Remember how much I love you. And think, Lil. Think how to avoid what we'll both surely regret.

"A retired lady in Dayton, Ohio, ignored this plea despite better judgment, and as a result she lost three fingers in a sausage grinder. Then repo crews came for her hatchback and condo. She lost her goldfish and she went blind in one eye. Then she sank into the underclass. This could happen to you. Worse could."

Can Lillian have suffered a stroke sitting in the afternoon shade? Or is this the big one, and in a few minutes will the faithful friend find the lap he lays his muzzle on cold, nobody home this time and nobody coming home either?

"I'm departing Key West with mixed feelings," confides Vola. She shoves on a sunbonnet, ties its straps under her chin, and nudges femme fatale sunglasses up the bridge of her nose with a thumb. "More than mixed, I don't know about you."

Scarcely dawn, trailer court parking lot smelling like a laundromat. Through palmettos poke lollipops, no, blossoms. Pigeons and sparrows drink at rosy puddles in the gravel.

Miami, Key West, Gunga-Munga, Manatee, the Everglades

"Everything stowed?" In an ocher coverall Vince stamps and slaps his arms. A rooster crows.

Tink in roomy camouflage and high-tops pads from the office as Denise in a green jumper trips down wobbly cinderblock steps with a picnic basket. "I whipped up a tropical compote to go with the flautas. Tink, help me get the top down."

"You got it. Six-packs icing? You girls wanna hop in the back? Vince, you take shotgun, I'm fresh as a daisy. One last cruise down Duval?"

In the still-dreaming Old Town, fringes of Spanish moss stir in a half-hearted good-bye. Out Truman, Roosevelt, past high-rises, electronics megaplexes and discount liquor. In the marina, masts caucus discreetly under a clear sky that grows larger and larger. The coupe bumps across to the next island, and on blackish piles canted out of the brine pelicans and anhingas watch, jaundiced, skeptical.

Returns always feel shorter. Island, bridge, island, bridge, east curving north, Gulf left and Atlantic right, two lanes on long bridges so traffic must rearrange on keys—so that, while the column advances steadily, speed is out of the question—so that, even with the top down, raised windows make the moving car a bowl of talk audible above seatbacks, talk bobbing on local radio salsa and sho-sho.

At Sugarloaf Key, in response to Tink's ribbing Vince about how much better love juices flow at these latitudes, Vola, relentless as an oboe, remarks that, whatever may have happened during Vince's nocturnal rambles, and much as she has enjoyed this getaway, and tried to maintain congeniality, in fact no love juices at all have flowed between her and Vince, nor will any. After an awkward silence Vince tells all and sundry, "Win some, lose some."

"Is that ever true," agrees Tink, and simultaneously Neesy is moved to note that things may have turned out for the best, and that sex isn't everything—last month she caught a talk show about happy sexless marriages—and she hopes Vola and Gramps remain friends because she and Tink will expect them both at the wedding.

"Picked a date?" asks Vola.

Neesy sighs. "Now that we can afford any time, I'm considering June. Would that be too soon?"

The roadway skips over waves from key to key through a sunny fresh morning, toward the mainland. Past Islamorada a speedboat curves ahead under the bridge and out into the Gulf.

"Whoops, that reminds me," says Vola. "We told you about the mêlée at the opera, Vince, but what with one thing and another I never got around to telling any of you about what I saw at sunset, when we all were playing round robin in the Mallory crowd."

"The housecat that jumped through a hoop of fire?" guesses Tink. "It only had five toes a paw, by the way. The trainer said the natives are too pampered to learn tricks. His is lean mean Jersey alley, four years old."

"Lucky to have even five toes," observes Vince. "I missed that myself."

Vola says, "Me too. What I saw is something else. At least I think I saw it. Everybody else was glued to the sunset but at the edge of the terrace I noticed three Papas had set up a weapon, to shoot toward the water."

"Doesn't surprise me," says Neesy. "I knew from the start something was fishy with that crowd."

Tink toots at a bathing beauty on a sailboat anchored below. "Drug money. Ask me, the whole Lookalike deal is a front. What went down at the opera proves it. Plus, the dude at Island Bicycles gave me a funny look when I told him I planned to come back next year as a contender myself."

Vola says, "I didn't want to be seen seeing the wrong thing, but I couldn't restrain my curiosity, and I still had the opera glasses. In the San Carlos confusion I'd forgotten to replace them."

"Probably set off alarms leaving the premises," says Tink. "But you had plenty of diversionary cover."

Vola chuckles. "I could FedEx them back. Between us, though, I may hang on to them as a souvenir, of this dip south and specifically of what I saw while the rest of you gawked at the sunset."

"Tell," says Denise.

"That speedboat reminded me. At first I thought the Hemingways were targeting a miniature speedboat, almost a toy. A concession, I supposed."

"Like carny ducks?"

"I couldn't tell, Tink, so I used the glasses and . . ." A catch interrupts Vola's whanging flow of words. Her fellow motorists stare. She swallows. "It wasn't a boat. More an outboard surfboard with a steering wheel. Papas were firing at the driver, and I recognized her. It was the woman from the opera, the Steinway in the box."

Tink nods. "The Hems were taking potshots at her there at the opera too."

"And apparently vice versa," adds Vince. "You saved her life at the opera, you said."

"Mmm," says Vola. "As things turned out, I wonder whether I might not better have kept my big mouth shut."

Neesy holds her places with a fingertip on a page in each of two ragged books open on her lap. "And let her actually die?"

Vola shrugs. "Then and there in her box instead of two hours later. Because they did pick her off in the water. She had banked, I suppose to return fire, and she took a hit. The board skittered on while she went under. Waving, screaming. I myself waved with my free hand and I screamed for somebody to rescue her. You remember what a crush it was, though. I was hemmed in, and anybody who noticed me must have thought I was celebrating sunset.

"I didn't want to lose the spot where she'd gone down, so I kept the glasses trained on it, but she never popped back up. All I saw were some bubbles." Wobbling up from the cruel bottom of the sea, soft as wine, disappearing as they surfaced. Vola clucks. "Given the choice, I think I'd have cashed in chips at the opera. Whatcha reading, Neesy? Two at once?"

"A bird book, for a spoonbill we just passed. But I was really reviewing our tour guide check marks. Tonight we need to stay in striking distance of a branch ATM where Tink and I pick up the last chain letter payments."

"In Miami?" asks Vince.

Vola glances at the drawing in Neesy's bird book. "Looks like Karl Malden," she says. "A character actor, used to act in commercials. For travelers' checks, come to think of it."

Neesy tells Vince, "Greater Miami. A town called Gunga-Munga."

"Seems to ring a bell," says Vince. "Maybe we should bed down there."

"How's the book scope it?" asks Tink.

Vince interrupts. "So even though your fat lady never sang at the opera, she went down belting out something in the Gulf. At all like Kate Smith?" He glances over his shoulder. "Don't bother explaining to the youngsters. But I was thinking about the dame that was on my case down there. She was ample too. Anybody hear anything about a weight-watchers' convention?"

Neesy looks up from her tour guide. "Most of the Papas needed to shed a few pounds."

"Not and remain authentic, dear," advises Vola.

"Not and stay contenders," adds Tink.

Vince says, "I was thinking, though. Wouldn't it be funny if we were all talking about the same broad. Funny ha-ha. It would mean she'd had a dose of poetic justice for how she treated me."

"Wouldn't let you into her pants?" Vola asks.

"Hers either?" adds Tink.

"Worse. She was using me for target practice. So you can see it would be appropriate if she was your surfer."

"We'll never know, Gramps."

"Not the way you mean," Vince concedes.

Vola shakes her head. "Whoever she was, she was too young to die that way."

Vince snorts. "So's everybody, but who cares?"

"Who cares, Gramps?"

Vince wipes his face with an open hand. "When I was a kid and my first pooch died, it broke my heart. I got a replacement, but he eventually died too. A street sweeper flattened the third one. His name was Annibale and he looked like he'd been stepped on by an elephant when I found him. By then, though, a process of induction had started to spare me grief."

"Just a dog, huh," suggests Tink.

Vince scratches the back of his head. "Not exactly. I remember we had a photo of Papa's father on the dining room wall in Brooklyn. He had a rifle and two Calabrian hunting dogs that Papa himself remembered by name. Lillian and I kept the picture. Your mother, Neesy, would remember it in the back hall. Sometimes when I looked at it I almost got tears in my eyes. But for the dogs, not the man.

"Because they had such a short time. What, four or five of their generations for one of ours? Plus, they didn't know the picture was being snapped." Yet standing still as the man, watching as obediently. Vince sighs. "People, dogs—you feel strange getting worked up when one of them shoots the rapids, when you stop to think how run of the mill it is."

"Same for most things," says Tink.

Miami, Key West, Gunga-Munga, Manatee, the Everglades

"Okay listen," Denise says. "'Gunga-Munga, with vintage ersatz Arabian architecture, offers a tantalizing glimpse into formative years of the south Florida tourist industry. Comfort and amusement practically for the asking.' Should we give it a whirl? Of course this must be out of date a little." She sniffs the book. "Or a lot."

The quartet reaches Miami in time for a late picnic lunch. At a park above white sand they find a pink table under a violet parasol. As far as the eye can see in either direction luxury hotels front the beach, each with its turquoise pool. Money and music seem to spill down vast glass faces, and nymphs and lesser potentates lean from balconies. Hovercraft glitter beyond the surf and on the horizon a dark liner ploughs open ocean northward, gone by the time Neesy serves her compote.

After a snooze on benches the four pile back into the coupe and proceed inland and north to Gunga-Munga. Vola casts an appraising eye at seedy cookie-cutter stucco cottages, tricycles, and peeling billboards. "Fifty-, sixty-year-old, rental for the past thirty. Multiple families in single-family units, massive code violation. Gang, this is underclass territory. You sure your bank is here?"

Neesy frowns. "I thought so. Where's downtown? You're right about the neighborhood. We could almost be home in Baltimore."

While Gunga-Munga looks only fractionally more promising along the approach to the business district, its architectural character does grow Hollywood Moorish, and pedestrian and automotive traffic increases, most headed in the same direction. "What's happening?" Tink asks a group of pedestrians making better time than the coupe.

"Fat Tuesday," says a middle-aged redhead with cat whiskers painted on her face. One of her companions wears a lampshade and the other, in an eye patch, carries a toy parrot. Everybody seems to wear a suggestion of a costume, as though weathered adults and skinny children alike have decided to play dress-up.

It soon becomes apparent that the bank and most other businesses have been closed since noon for the holiday, and since Gunga-Munga seems to be nearing gridlock, Tink slips into a parking deck whose attendant assures the out-of-towners that their car will be safe, they can find rooms in the adjoining hotel, and banks will open in the morning.

Neesy and Tink order the President's wing, three connecting street-front suites on the third, and top, floor, with the best view for street festivities, which should be more lively than usual tonight, the desk clerk confides. In the cramped rickety elevator, its champagne walls filmed with tobacco and who knows what else, in response to Vola's effusions of gratitude Neesy confides, "Actually it wasn't much of a splurge, unless they only billed us for one room by mistake. Not even then, in fact."

The four freshen up and enjoy gin and tonics in the youngsters' suite, the middle one, with magic fingers even in its love sea, and an autographed snapshot of the Truman family. After dinner in the hotel's underground restaurant featuring junk salads and a dessert cart loaded with babas au rhum, it's time to return to the suite for a spell on the balcony in the dank evening. Nameless Gunga-Mungans carouse beneath minarets and domes, and with their feeble laughter, garbage can lids, jugs, and other muffled noisemakers they make a monotonous and even soothing protomusic that persists past bedtime and into dreams.

In the morning Tink leaves his companions at café con leche while he makes a run to the bank. The only other breakfaster, a Miami human-affairs journalist, strikes up a conversation and explains that he has never seen the Gunga-Munga Mardi Gras so lively. Scarcely has he mounted the stairs when down trudges a now glum Tink.

"Not open yet?" asks Vince.

"Not another bank failure," says Vola.

Neesy searches Tink's face. "It's serious, guys," she concludes. "We'll survive, Tinks. Don't pull that scowl, you'll give me heartburn."

Tink sits on the stairway. "You're not going to believe this." Although the chain letter balance arrived yesterday, because of a combination of human and electronic error the sum was dispersed to the Gunga-Munga citizenry before noon, a windfall that explains their increased merry-making. "The teller said it's irretrievable. Underclass parties up and down the coast will have blown most of our stash already. He said we might recover something if we took it to court. Dream on, pal, I felt like saying. We're on the drafty side of the law ourselves." Silence.

More silence. Neesy says, "It was only two thirds. We're still loaded. Let's see how it plays. Worse comes to worst, we do another letter."

Miami, Key West, Gunga-Munga, Manatee, the Everglades

Silence, Vince and Vola examining crumbs on the table, Tink his shoelaces, while Neesy holds a straight-ahead "Why not?" face as if to allow a video camera time to cut away.

"Okay," says Tink. "We're young enough to roll with the punches."

"There you go," says Vince. "It's not your fault, either."

"It was their money," Vola can't help saying.

"In a manner of speaking," adds Vince quickly. He waves his arms and claps his hands. "Let's get this show on the road, by cracky." As Gabby Hayes he continues, "Ol' Manatee's a-yodelin' to me, little doggies, and dang nab it, this buckaroo's had escapades enough for this pertic'lar roundup."

Spirits rise as the convertible leaves Greater Miami and enters the Everglades on the Tamiami Trail. "Speaking of escapades, Gramps. You still owe us the clincher of your manhunt. Or rather theirs for you. How you wound up at sunset," Neesy says, at the wheel, with Tink shotgun.

Vince sits behind her, an arm across the seat back like a

pterodactyl's wing sheltering Vola. "The more I cogitate, the more a little bird tells me my would-be assassin must have been the dame you saw drown, Vola. I mean, what are the odds? Unless they were running some kind of auxiliary with the Hemingways, Steinway Lookalikes for a Mamas and Papas Day. Where was I?"

Vola says, "On the beach road, the night before you showed up at Mallory. The mystery woman. Let's call her Gertrude, by the way. She was solid, all right, assuming yours was the same as ours, but Steinway really presents an unfair picture. She was pursuing you."

"The Trolls," interjects Tink. "You'd left them. Or was it the Deadheads?"

"Both."

"Wait," says Vola. "Weren't some of them in the opera fracas?"

Neesy nods. "Now that you mention it. Are they in the drug wars too?"

"Search me," says Tink. "Look, conveniences ahead. I don't know about you guys but my bladder's bursting from all that con leche."

Miami, Key West, Gunga-Munga, Manatee, the Everglades

At the deserted rest stop the coupe parks under a catalpa flowering beside the canal, and its occupants stroll pair by pair into each side of the lichenous cinderblock. When the women exit they find the men lounging against the car. Vola says, "Ours wasn't as well maintained as it should have been. How was yours?"

Vince shakes his head. "Oh, you know."

Neesy frowns. "I hope you two haven't been smoking in the boys' room."

"Or telling secrets," adds Vola. "Say, wonder where that path leads. It follows the canal into the pines, but I can't tell if the land beyond has been cleared. Think I'll have a look, if you don't mind. Shouldn't take five minutes."

"We'll come too, won't we, boys?"

"Lead on, Pathfinder," Vince tells Vola. "I'll guard the rear."

Indian-file, the procession marches alongside the dun water. Purple cumulus towers in the southwest sky, and gusts curvet among pines and palmettos, in marsh grass, lifting queer wet-dry smells, like a handful of raindrops brushing hot tin, like a mulch transition where papery leaves darken toward decomposition. Neesy with her bird book advises that a leafless silver tree's zany coiffure houses ospreys, not eagles.

As they walk, Vince continues his account of how back on the Key West beach road he left the Trolls, saw Deadheads gathered in the distance, and pedaled his purloined velocipede to ignition when he lost consciousness for what must have been a good half hour. As he revived in the streaming moonlight he seemed to recall an explosion, and his mount bucking under him. Had it been wired with a plastique?

No, the poor thing lay on its side, quiet and entire, across the road from where he lay, unable, he discovered, to move more than head, toes, and fingers. When a young couple of lovers passed, his faint cries failed to distract them. He watched them stroll on toward the Old Town. A cyclist with a parrot on his shoulder wheeled by too, silent down the road.

Was Vince bleeding? With each breath pain and numbness flowered from his breastbone. He lost consciousness again. Light through lids and a whiff of smelling salts brought him to, as a public safety officer on night patrol summoned a medivac team who eased him onto a stretcher, into a van that rushed him to an emergency room. "You've been shot in the chest," explained an orderly, "but your vitals are good. Minimal blood loss."

Vince cackles. "No loss, in fact. By mid-morning they'd figured it out, and also I could move. They'd stuck me for pain and I was ready to roll, but they wanted to keep me another hour. I dozed off and it turned into four or five hours.

"I considered ringing up Murtry's in case anybody was worried, but if I said where I was calling from you'd come after me, and there was a sympathetic nurse I thought I might get somewhere with. Would have, too, except they threw me out to handle an OIDS case."

Tink says, "Tough luck, Vince."

Denise, second in line, asks over her shoulder, "But what had happened to you, Gramps?"

"A miracle. I'd been shot for sure and Gertrude must have done it. They found the bullet in my navel and the officer said it came from an antique lady's gat. The bullet was flattened, but he could tell. This flattened it. Look."

Vince's audience complies, having reached a fork where the path widens. Vince fishes from a breast pocket and displays between a thumb and forefinger what at first looks to be a zinc brooch with yellow cloisonné and dark bright settings. "It's the amulet the Babalaw sold me. The car. I had it in my shirt pocket and it stopped the bullet." Vince looks up at his spectators.

Expecting to see wonder or disbelief on three faces, Vince in fact sees horror. Pointing fingers, urgent waving hands signal. Vince hears his granddaughter make drowning noises, "G-g-gr-gr," until she manages "G-Gramps!" Vola and Tink shout, "Run!" What the . . . ? Now Vince realizes that the brushy noise behind him has increased, and a new smell has arisen, sour and soapy. Look behind you, Vince.

Clambering forward, flither thunk-flither, grunting, between squashing clawed pads a vast low face, pale under jaw, teeth and more teeth around the snout, nostrils and intent eyes erected.

Run, old Vince, run behind companions away from the water to the rest stop and coupe, into which jump all four, slam doors, count heads and Tink locate keys, ignition, exit. Lay down rubber.

Vola first recovers voice a good minute west on the Tamiami Trail. "I thought you were a goner, Vince. You okay?"

Vince inhales. "I may need a hand when we get to Manatee. I'm no spring chicken."

Tink laughs. "All the same, that's one disappointed croc."

"Or gator," says Neesy. "Both live here. Let me check the reptile book, in the side pocket there. Gramps, I'll bet you dropped your lucky charm. Should we go back for it?"

Vince shudders.

"Never mind," advises Vola. "It's given you your money's worth. Twice over now, you might say."

Tink says, "That reminds me, Vince. Will you notify the Key West authorities they can call off their search for Gertrude, unless they want to drag the Gulf?"

"Nahh. When they took the report I could see they didn't expect to spend many taxpayers' dollars on the investigation. Anyway I didn't give my right name. Didn't want to be bothered."

Neesy says, "Guess I didn't get a good enough look to say which reptile it was." She hands the book over her shoulder.

"Whichever," says Tink, "his stomach must be rumbling now. That dude was licking his lips, Vince."

"Do alligators have lips?" asks Neesy.

"Do crocodiles have tongues?" adds Vola.

Past the fringes of the great swamp the orange coupe bounces into the thickening traffic and tangled interchanges of Tampa Bay.

THREE

Manatee

Brent eases the Runkle limo into diffused shade under the palm leaning out between Manatee Curios and Videos and the Village Mortuary. He extends sensors and jockeys into position within an inch of the curb. Not that either traffic officer would bat an eye to find the well-known and properly registered vehicle a smidgin farther out, but of late Brent, always meticulous, feels still more inclined to cross the t and dot the i.

Gwen in her bucket seat might be regarding her manicure, ogives glistening in a frosted nude along the ends of the tiny hands she has laid like a raccoon's on her lap. Since the brim of her straw cloche lies against her cheek Brent can only guess at the direction of her gaze. Perhaps she has simply bowed her head and closed her eyes.

Not to worry, she has advised, caressing his shoulders and also somehow monitoring, through the embroidered rayon of the Elvis shirt he has chosen for its high collar. As the lab report due date passes, and another day, not to worry. Brent switches off the ignition. Not worry. Today provides some distraction, however sad and even shameful, in the unspoken memory of an only child's christening on this date decades ago, and there may also be relief and distraction in the Manatee "Library."

Locks and alarms set—who can be sure of anything, these days, even in Manatee?—Brent trots around for Gwen's door. Inside in a cubicle Brent tells a terminal, "Reference, please." He and Gwen relax on an extruded sofa.

Brent finds Gwen's ear and mutters, "Wouldn't you like to take charge? When I'm at the helm, too much gets bleeped. This place gives me the willies. I'd rather be swimming laps or golfing."

Gwen whispers, "Don't you get those willies, Brentsy." Then loudly she enters the reference continuum with, "We'd like to know what's available in electronic mirrors and enhancers. Programs that might permit the viewer to see herself as others see her, for instance, by flipping the image, if you see what I mean. End of request."

"We forgot user friendliness," Brent whispers as a wash of talk and images begins.

The subject proves more interesting than the Runkles expected, for there are mirrors to accelerate or reverse age, and trick mirrors such as those showing viewers nude. While some of these sound worth ordering on approval, the Runkles resist enticements as they negotiate electronic ladders and trapezes to arrive at the desired information. Wafer-thin electronic mirrors offer reversal together with enhanced definition so that, should the double-wide's anomalous electric field continue to reverse clock hands, these mirrors, judiciously placed, might effect corrections. Faces without numerals will read as before. With others the eye should quickly learn to read, say, a reversed Arabic seven as a five. Roman numerals, potentially more confusing because five vertically symmetrical ones in the dozen fail to register reversal, in time should come around as well.

Before exiting reference Brent inquires about the search for an OIDS cure. The network hiccups and remarks that handgun sales are up in many parts of the world. "See," Brent whispers into Gwen's ear, "I can never make it do what I want. Let's split before I get the creeps." When the opening door invites patrons to hurry on back, he adds, "I miss people. In the old days when you came to a place like this you saw actual people, didn't you? Back when there was hard copy?"

Crossing the lane ahead of him Gwen muses, "They became flophouses. Remember?"

He nods and opens her door. As she slides in, he observes, "Even sleepers keep being people, though."

There should be time before dinner for a rest. Tyge wags his "tail" in the entry, and the substitute mail carrier seems late again today. In the subdued horizontal light of the bedroom Brent blushes at new blotches he uncovers when he strips to skivvies before easing himself onto the satin comforter. Purring, Gwen crosses to her powder room, where she slips into a liquid peignoir and dusts her face and arms with a nacreous distillate of sweet almonds, vanilla, and tuberoses. In a conventional mirror she mouths, "Be strong."

Abed side-by-side like dolls on the gleaming expanse the Runkles meditate, and perhaps doze, for when the bedroom carillon peals six they rise to discover that the mail has arrived. "Bills and junk," Gwen says. "Except, ah, here we are." She hands over an official envelope.

Brent hands it back. "Would you mind?"

As she slits the envelope and extracts and shakes the page open and reads, Brent fears to watch her face, and yet he does, and sees her eyes widen and then narrow. She seems lost in thought until, recovering, she shakes her head and passes Brent the report. Not breathing, he skims the preamble, the hedges and the telephone numbers, down to the sentence with blanks, the first of which contains his name. "Please be informed that the result of your HOHO test is . . ."

In the second blank, where Brent hoped to read "Negative" or "Good," and feared to read the opposite, he sees an ink spot large enough to hide any of the envisioned words. "An accident," he concludes. "We'll have to call. Just our luck."

Gwen approaches a window. "Mr. Margiotta seems to be out. Hopefully with that ratty granddaughter and the boyfriend she must have rescued from an animal shelter."

Brent dons a neckerchief. "Probably driven to Tampa for dinner. The youngsters head north tomorrow, Vince said."

Even as Brent speaks, however, Vince, Neesy and Tink, and Lillian too, sit in Manatee itself, in Neptune's bar. A more lavish dinner would have made no dent in the youngsters' new budget, but Vince has insisted that this be his treat. Furthermore, as Neesy has confided to Tink, she prefers to spend this last Manatee evening with Gramps in a regular haunt of his. The party has left its name on the waiting list for one of Neptune's coveted booths.

According to the *Ebbtide*, Neptune's Locker with its blue lava lamps and undersea treasure motif adds much to an evening's pleasure at the popular cafeteria. Erstwhile windows have become tropical aquaria whose brilliant denizens hang motionless before flickering into another stasis. Can they see through the glass? Surely they can't hear the carioca medley, the ice the barkeep shakes like dice, or the voices.

Lillian has agreed to this outing with some sense of biting the bullet. It seemed only right to accord this one meeting with a daughter's daughter and her beau. With pleasant enough memories of Denise as moppet, Lillian supposes she could coast through the evening on automatic if not for Vince, flirting with his jokes and tales of adventure in the Keys, and planning to drop off the youngsters after dinner before driving Lil to her trailerette for another heroic try at her, doubtless.

With drinks and a pu-pu platter, and some corn nuts for the men to toss into their mouths, the party surveys the menu. Tonight's specials include local possum baked with sweet potatoes. "They come out of the swamp," Vince explains. "Greasy meat, but not bad. Some of them may be roadkill. They used to call me Possum when I was a boy."

"Because you were a pest?" asks Neesy. "Because I can't see you playing possum."

After a few minutes the women retire to the ladies' room where on a sofa they consider each other more frankly, and Neesy opens matters of consequence. "Gramps seems lost, and I wonder what it would hurt for you to take him back, assuming you can take pity. Not that it's my business, except that I love the old guy. Always did, and more now."

"Under advisement," says Lillian. "That's the best I can offer. Except also this. It's just me. It doesn't have anything to do with your grandpa, Neesy. And certainly not with you and your Tink. If I weren't superstitious I'd say your future looks rosy to me."

"Thanks. We plan to see you in Baltimore soon. We'll put you and Vince up in separate suites or together. Shall we get back to the boys?"

The Locker has filled some now. Lillian and Neesy return to their table, and conversation resumes, about Manatee demographics. Having been founded half a century ago with the unspoken (indeed unconscious) assumption that only middle-to-lower-middle-class heterosexual Wasps would find the community attractive, by now even the most inert variable, class, has begun to fluctuate, in both directions.

Talk turns to the road trip the youngsters will begin in the morning. They have sent the bulk of their fortune ahead electronically, observing more precautions than with Gunga-Munga, yet they will travel with enough cash to make Vince and Lillian enjoin weather eyes on freeways infested with serial murderers, terrorists, and convoys of arms, drugs, and hazardous waste. Tink has bought a money belt to wear under briefs with the family jewels.

Now Gwen Runkle glides in, followed by Brent dancing like a marionette. Lillian notices them and for a moment loses her bearings, for they seem in partial mourning. Both wear charcoal and lavender darkened by the Locker's blue light. Gwen wears a retro femme fatale black veil with spots of black velvet like beauty marks. Lillian looks away wondering, could Brent also have such a veil, or was it only an after-image? And wasn't their annual parental mourning a week or two ago? Gwen meanwhile without moving her lips tells Brent sotto voce how disappointing it is to catch Lillian in capitulation like this after all Gwen's efforts to the contrary.

Waves, nods, and after Brent has left the Runkle name on the waiting list for booths, he and Gwen pause at the Margiotta table. Lillian sees that Brent's apparent spotted veil in fact consists of dermatological irregularities, which she also now notices on the backs of his hands. Comments on weather, on Pepito's reliability even with possum, some casting about for other topics. "Ah!" Gwen exclaims. "Lillian, I've been dying to tell you!" She presses her small moist hands together. "You'll never imagine what my Brent found us for an anniversary gift!"

"Tyge," says Lillian. "You told me, remember?" She enjoys the little triumph. "How's he working out? He is a he, isn't he?"

Tink shoots Neesy a look, what's your grandma talking about? Neesy shakes her head, no clue, no matter. Inky ringlets wave across her white brow and over her ears.

Gwen says, "Of course," and, retaliating, continues, "Just the other day, wasn't it? When you met Pepito in the garden. Tyge is a dream. He'll have to meet your flesh and blood pooch. Really, they're working electronic miracles, aren't they, Brent? Tell what we learned today."

"Learned?"

"At the 'Library.' You recall."

As Brent recapitulates the afternoon's research, and beside him Gwen's head rocks in nearly insensible encouragement, her eyelids lowered, and most of the rest of Brent's audience's lids settle to half mast, Lillian alone listens with care, because it seems that these foolish Runkles may be dealing her a trump card. Brent concludes, "Questions?" and Lillian is about to put several when a loud voice interrupts. A leggy waitress in French roll, frilly white blouse, short black shift, fishnets, and black patent heels high enough to make her need to lean down to pore over the wait list announces, "Booths. Denny, party of two. This way please. Also Marquette, party of four. Marquette?"

"We were the first quartet," says Lillian, standing. Then she fears she said something quite different, for her tablemates, as if rooted to their seats, stare each at the other two in wonder, for they all recognize the honking voice (which now stirs something in Lillian's own memory) of the waitress who turns to say, "Last call for Marquette."

Tink leaps to his feet. "Vola! That's Margiotta, girl. Wipe your specs."

Vola shoves menus into the Dennys' hands and shoos them to the dining room before stepping over to her friends' table. "Hi, there." Snapping gum, pencil behind an ear, she introduces herself to the Runkles.

"We've heard of you," allows Gwen.

"The caboose lady," offers Vola.

Butter wouldn't melt in Vince's mouth as he introduces Vola and Lillian, for he has found himself in similar situations before. Still, the reactions he sees almost warrant a double take. Lampblack and Windex eyes meet as in recognition, and gravely. Each woman takes the other's hand.

Tink says, "So, Vola, you make good tips with those stockings? We didn't know you planned to wait tables."

"A girl's gotta eat. I saw an *Ebbtide* ad and thought, why not give it a whirl, what better place for a gold digger? The fishnets carry out of the marine theme. At least I thought so before tonight."

"?"

"Well." Vola strikes a confidential pose, knuckles on hip. "As you may know, Manatee's upstanding Pepito Gutierrez has a shady past. South of the border, shall we say. Second-generation Cali cartel."

"They were the kinder gentler ones," muses Denise. "Or was that Medellín?"

Vola pushes a stray lock into place and secures it with a bobby pin she has opened against incisors. "Search me, kid. For the line of work, though, they seem to have treated him okay. They let him buy out and adopt a new identity."

"Mid-life lifestyle renovation," suggests Tink. He looks up from his menu and taps it. "What do you recommend, Vola? Enough parsley here?"

"There is now," says Vola. "Let's see. Pretty routine tonight, except I wouldn't advise the triggerfish. Parsley makes all the difference with possum, by the way."

Gwen clears her throat. "You were saying, Miss Byrd. About Pepito?"

"Righto. They let him put himself out to pasture but they keep tabs, and I suppose from time to time they might retain him as a consultant."

"All this," says Lillian, "we never dreamed about Pepito. No flies on you, Vola."

"A single working girl keeps her ear to the ground if she's wise. So where was I? Oh yes, an old associate of Pepito's dropped in tonight. When I glimpsed her disappearing into his office I started to wonder, because she seemed to have fishnets too. What do you suppose it could mean?"

"Could?" wonders Vince, although neither he nor anyone else replies.

Vola continues, "You folks must be hungry. Mr. and Ms. Runkle, you shouldn't have much of a wait." To let the Margiotta quartet precede her, Vola steps aside and then freezes, staring toward the entrance. "My stars, there they are now." Pepito and his guest cross the threshold. "But wait," continues the new waitress. "Wait, wait."

Vola looks as if she's seen a ghost, Lillian thinks, yet Pepito, or whatever his real name is, nods and smiles in a thoroughly unghostly manner as he ushers his guest this way. Fishnet hose? No, it looks more like argyle knee socks with her Earth shoes. She too seems entirely, even overly, corporeal in her Bolivian peasant costume, striding forward with no trace of the delicacy some heavy women affect.

Lillian glances aside to see whether anyone else has noticed Vola Byrd's odd demeanor. Poor Lillian, set to pooh-pooh, finds herself taken aback by what she now sees. Not only Vola but also Lillian's three tablemates, and also the two Runkles, all gape alike.

The large woman stops, and stops Pepito with a hand on his shoulder. He seems uncomprehending but suave. Across two yards of sandy carpet the two and the seven puzzle each other in an ultramarine zone that distances bar chatter and clink, a crooner's lover standing on golden sands watching ships go sailing.

Then Brent cries, "Ruby!" and Tink says, "It's Gertrude, back from a muddy death." Pepito meanwhile tells his customers and waitress that he would like to present his old friend Carmencita. Vola stands like a moose in headlights. Merrily merrily tinkles cocktail piano, merrily merrily, life is but a dream.

At last the woman speaks. "Papa. Mama," she tells Brent and Gwen. "Funny how chance works, funny strange. I thought we'd never see one another again. I've often regretted how I left you, and once I even tried to track you down.

If you can forgive me, do. And Papa, whatever treatment they've prescribed for the condition I regret seeing you with is hoodoo, but I just may have what the doctor ordered. It's new, it's contraband, and it works in three cases out of ten. You and Mother might better call me Carmen, my legal name now, legal as anything about me. I've used other aliases, but Gertrude must be somebody else. If you prefer Ruby for old time's sake, no problem. I've let a few intimates call me that over the years.

"I didn't expect ever to see you again either," she tells Vola. "I recognize you from Key West and I owe you my life. I don't know how to repay you, but please receive my undying gratitude before these witnesses. Your young friends seem familiar also, and now I recall seeing them in the balcony with you that fateful night at the opera."

Turning to the Margiottas, Carmen continues, "You seem the only ones here whose paths have never crossed mine. Or initiated mine," she says with a glance to the Runkles. "Although you, sir," she continues, turning back toward Vince, "resemble a gentleman whose machinations I recently ended. Also in Key West, as it happens."

"Machinations?"

"Would-be muscling in. Run of the mill for a narcotics queen."

"King, Neesy and I thought," remarks Tink. "In Key West we took Carmen to be Italian, and supposed you were a godfather."

As Vince considers saying or asking more, Vola finds her voice. "After I watched you go down in the Gulf at sunset the day after the opera I didn't expect to see you again dead or alive. You're not a zombie, are you?"

Neesy says, "Maybe when she drowned she was wearing a Santeria car."

"Whatever you mean," says Carmen, "that was one of my closer shaves. I'm Papa's girl though. I've always been a good swimmer, and a silicone-hemoglobin oxygen exchanger allowed me to breathe water and not surface before circling the piers.

"I had goggles and I saw fluorescent yellow and blue angelfish, striped sergeant majors, and yellow-orange parrots with black lipstick and blue eye shadow, but who knows what marine carnivores lurked there too? When I stepped onto land again, on my wrist I found a small octopus."

Gwen clasps hands and lays them against a shoulder like a rapt saint. "Our very daughter."

"That's right," says Carmen. "Then and there I decided to call it quits while there was still time. I remembered Pepito, and came to discuss my plans with him. I had not meant to stay in Manatee more than a few hours, but now that I see you all I would not like to leave so soon, if my parents can find pardon in their hearts."

"We can," says Brent. "No, dear?"

Through closed lids Gwen seems to measure the large daughter before her. "Absolutely."

Vola says, "Yes, you ought to stay a while. In fact, why don't you move here? I could help you find a place. Before waitressing I sold real estate. Unless you prefer to stay liquid. Or, even then. Listen, sugar, why not join your parents for dinner. Their booth should have opened. When I get off work, I'll show you my fixer-upper. Cute as a bug's ear. You can even sleep over. Your folks won't mind, and you can see their double-wide tomorrow. It'll show to best advantage by the light of day. Whatcha say?"

"Thank you. This will prove a pleasure."

* * *

Part Three

At the blue trailer on Dockside Lillian says good-bye to the youngsters, who plan to depart before dawn. "I'll be up but not presentable. Drive carefully, and take care of each other. I know you will." Hugs and kisses. See one another soon in Baltimore.

Vince drives Lillian home in his pickup, near midnight, trailers dark, clement air, the old moon in the new moon's arms. Neither tries to speak over the wheezing and rattling of the truck. Lillian has left a light in her trailerette and you can see Cerbero's head bounce at a window and hear him when Vince kills the engine.

"I got him while you were in Key West. Thought I should have a watchdog even in Manatee, nowadays." Lillian chuckles voicelessly. "I had another reason too. I plain wanted a dog. We never had one, and I didn't have one as a kid either."

Vince crosses his arms on the steering wheel, lays his head on his arms, and looks at his wife. "Did you ask? Your parents, I mean? I don't think you suggested it to me, although one of the girls must have. But jeez, Lillian, I have nothing against dogs. I could convert the tool shed into a doghouse."

Lillian shakes her head. "I'm not blaming anybody. I

didn't even know I wanted one myself. I don't know how long it will last either. Maybe tomorrow I'll have had enough dog."

Vince watches and waits.

"I'm humoring myself. I guess that's it."

"Did you read my letters?"

Lillian turns to rest her back against the door. "Were you in shock from Carmen's assault when you wrote the last one? It didn't seem entirely coherent."

Cerbero has stopped barking but his face continues to bob at the window. Vince says, "So what's the story?"

Lillian shakes her head. "I'm not coming back. Till death do us part? Okay, fair enough. What else is parting us now? I'm easy, Vince, I can put up with lots. Your two-timing, that dickhead in your drawers. I could learn not to notice what age keeps doing to us both, and you know I don't hold any grudges against you worth mentioning. You know I'm thankful for the Brooklyn years and for these Florida ones. The marriage, the girls, Neesy and the other grandchildren. We couldn't have done it without you, caro mio. I might want to live with you forever, were eternal life in the cards. However."

He shuts his eyes.

"About meaning vows, Vince. I think it depends on what they themselves mean. Till death do us part? It's a non-starter. Death parts us from day one, regardless of the stories we tell. When you jump out of the World Trade Center holding hands, okay, sure, lots of stories help in lots of circumstances. So what else is new? For me now there's no future in complicity, is all." Deep down, the valley's never been other than lonesome, caro mio.

Vince rests his brow on his forearms. "Don't say any more about it, Lillian."

After a moment Lillian says, "Only one or two things. You keep the Brooklyn plot for yourself or give it to somebody. I'll make my arrangements. No, my mind's made up. For the will I'll write, don't worry, it won't shame you if I go first. I don't expect to leave debts, but you won't be liable."

Vince bumps his brow against his forearm. "Have a heart, Lillian. Enough."

"Okay then. What the Runkles were talking about earlier, electronic wizardry, remember?"

Vince nods.

"It made me think, with all the virtual technology and so forth . . ."

Vince sits back, smoothing his hair and brightening. "They'll be happy you're not coming back to me. She anyway."

"I know. But what they made me wonder is, whether it might be possible to make a simulacrum of a person. A virtual person."

"What the hell are you talking about, Lillian?"

"I was wondering whether, if somebody wants a person to hang out with him, and the person knows it's time for her to strike out on her own . . ."

"Forget it. You're talking Bride of Frankenstein. Anyhow it wouldn't be feasible in time for us. In time for me."

"I'm not so sure. What I was thinking about would be in your mind."

"Forget about it, Lil."

"Okay. Look, it's not as though we'll be living at the opposite ends of the earth. Want a nightcap?"

"You need your beauty sleep. I'll sit here a spell though, maybe catch a few winks myself here rather than wake half of Manatee up with this junk heap. Don't worry if you look out and see me sitting with my eyes closed and not moving."

"Okay, Vince." She wouldn't be able to see whether his eyes were open anyway, from inside. "Good night."

"Good night, Lillian."

Minutes after dawn Vince pilots his jalopy home to Dockside Lane. The kids have stowed luggage and souvenirs, rations, maps, bird books and tour guides, and wind- and sunscreen, along with a fuzz buster, mace, and flares. "Gramps! We were starting to think about giving you a call. Everything okay?"

"Sure," says Vince. "You?"

"Set to roll," says Tink. "That reminds me. We demolished one of your window shades last night."

"How'd you happen to do that?"

"Nothing kinky, Gramps. When Tink pulled it down for modesty's sake, it fell apart."

Tink adds, "Shouldn't be a problem to replace. We'll ship you one down."

Vince shrugs. "Doesn't matter. Dry rot. The whole trailer's older than it was meant to last. Drive carefully, kids.

Too bad Vola didn't make it by for your departure. I thought she said something about it."

"She did, Gramps." Neesy glances at Tink.

Tink says, "Vola may be otherwise occupied. The way she and Carmen cottoned to each other last night, maybe you didn't strike out in Key West exactly the way you thought."

"That's right, Gramps. In my book it goes down as a TKO. See you in Baltimore."

"Right you are. Okay, bon voyage." Vince hugs each youngster and waves them off out of sight around the corner. At length they go out of earshot.

Time passes, and as the story closes early arrivals for Saturday morning social dancing at the Manatee senior citizens' center wait for Lillian Margiotta, or somebody, with a door key card. Like revenants on benches under palms they nod, inquire, and cluck about weather, 301KS, WMDS, futures, pacemakers, descendants, obits.

Did you hear how the long-lost daughter of the couple in the custom double-wide appeared on their doorstep? She's tied the knot with the caboose woman and is bankrolling her in a juice bar and target practice range scheduled to open next month. They're waiting for a double-wide to open up. Runkle's OIDS seems to have gone into remission as mysteriously as it appeared. The Runkles' neighbor Margiotta used to be married to Lillian, who's uncharacteristically late, if she's who we're waiting for. Come to think of it, didn't old Vince set sail coupla weeks back? Margiotta? Nahh, he'll outlive us all. You must have somebody else in mind.